DEAD MEN TELL NO TALES

Tumbling helter-skelter aboard the lowered long-boat.

DEAD MEN
TELL NO TALES

BY

E. W. HORNUNG

ILLUSTRATED BY
HARVEY T. DUNN

Fredonia Books
Amsterdam, The Netherlands

Dead Men Tell no Tales

by
E. W. Hornung

ISBN: 1-58963-941-3

Reprinted from the 1910 edition

Fredonia Books
Amsterdam, The Netherlands
http://www.fredoniabooks.com

In order to make original editions of historical works available to scholars at an economical price, this facsimile of the original edition of 1910 is reproduced from the best available copy and has been digitally enhanced to improve legibility, but the text remains unaltered to retain historical authenticity.

CONTENTS

Contents

ILLUSTRATIONS

Dead Men Tell No Tales

CHAPTER I

LOVE ON THE OCEAN

NOTHING is so easy as falling in love on a long sea voyage, except falling out of love. Especially was this the case in the days when the wooden clippers did finely to land you in Sydney or in Melbourne under the four full months. We all saw far too much of each other, unless, indeed, we were to see still more. Our superficial attractions mutually exhausted, we lost heart and patience in the disappointing strata which lie between the surface and the bed-rock of most natures. My own experience was confined to the round voyage of the *Lady Jermyn,* in the year 1853. It was no common experience, as was only too well known at the time. And I may add that I for my part had not the faintest intention of falling in love on board; nay, after all these years, let me confess that I had good cause to hold myself proof against

1

such weakness. Yet we carried a young lady,
coming home, who, God knows, might have made
short work of many a better man!

Eva Denison was her name, and she cannot
have been more than nineteen years of age. I
remember her telling me that she had not yet
come out, the very first time I assisted her to
promenade the poop. My own name was still unknown to her, and yet I recollect being quite fascinated by her frankness and self-possession. She
was exquisitely young, and yet ludicrously old for
her years; had been admirably educated, chiefly
abroad, and, as we were soon to discover, possessed accomplishments which would have made
the plainest old maid a popular personage on board
ship. Miss Denison, however, was as beautiful
as she was young, with the bloom of ideal health
upon her perfect skin. She had a wealth of lovely
hair, with strange elusive strands of gold among
the brown, that drowned her ears (I thought we
were to have that mode again?) in sunny ripples;
and a soul greater than the mind, and a heart
greater than either, lay sleeping somewhere in the
depths of her grave, gray eyes.

We were at sea together so many weeks. I cannot think what I was made of then!

It was in the brave old days of Ballarat and

2

Love on the Ocean

Bendigo, when ship after ship went out black with passengers and deep with stores, to bounce home with a bale or two of wool, and hardly hands enough to reef topsails in a gale. Nor was this the worst; for not the crew only, but, in many cases, captain and officers as well, would join in the stampede to the diggings; and we found Hobson's Bay the congested asylum of all manner of masterless and deserted vessels. I have a lively recollection of our skipper's indignation when the pilot informed him of this disgraceful fact. Within a fortnight, however, I met the good man face to face upon the diggings. It is but fair to add that the *Lady Jermyn* lost every officer and man in the same way, and that the captain did obey tradition to the extent of being the last to quit his ship. Nevertheless, of all who sailed by her in January, I alone was ready to return at the beginning of the following July.

I had been to Ballarat. I had given the thing a trial. For the most odious weeks I had been a licensed digger on Black Hill Flats; and I had actually failed to make running expenses. That, however, will surprise you the less when I pause to declare that I have paid as much as four shillings and sixpence for *half* a loaf of execrable bread; that my mate and I, between us, seldom

3

Dead Men Tell No Tales

took more than a few pennyweights of gold-dust
in any one day; and never once struck pick into
nugget, big or little, though we had the mortification of inspecting the "mammoth masses" of which
we found the papers full on landing, and which
had brought the gold-fever to its height during
our very voyage. With me, however, as with
many a young fellow who had turned his back on
better things, the malady was short-lived. We
expected to make our fortunes out of hand, and
we had reckoned without the vermin and the villainy which rendered us more than ever impatient
of delay. In my fly-blown blankets I dreamt of
London until I hankered after my chambers and
my club more than after much fine gold. Never
shall I forget my first hot bath on getting back to
Melbourne; it cost five shillings, but it was worth
five pounds, and is altogether my pleasantest remi-
niscence of Australia.

There was however, one slice of luck in store
for me. I found the dear old *Lady Jermyn* on the
very eve of sailing, with a new captain, a new
crew, a handful of passengers (chiefly steerage),
and nominally no cargo at all. I felt none the less
at home when I stepped over her familiar side.

In the cuddy we were only five, but a more un-
even quintette I defy you to convene. There was

4

Love on the Ocean

a young fellow named Ready, packed out for his health, and hurrying home to die among friends. There was an outrageously lucky digger, another invalid, for he would drink nothing but champagne with every meal and at any minute of the day, and I have seen him pitch raw gold at the sea-birds by the hour together. Miss Denison was our only lady, and her step-father, with whom she was travelling, was the one man of distinction on board. He was a Portuguese of sixty or thereabouts, Senhor Joaquin Santos by name; at first it was incredible to me that he had no title, so noble was his bearing; but very soon I realized that he was one of those to whom adventitious honors can add no lustre. He treated Miss Denison as no parent ever treated a child, with a gallantry and a courtliness quite beautiful to watch, and not a little touching in the light of the circumstances under which they were travelling together. The girl had gone straight from school to her step-father's estate on the Zambesi, where, a few months later, her mother had died of the malaria. Unable to endure the place after his wife's death, Senhor Santos had taken ship to Victoria, there to seek fresh fortune with results as indifferent as my own. He was now taking Miss Denison back to England, to make her home with other relatives, before he himself returned to Africa (as he once told me) to lay his bones beside those of his wife. I hardly know which of the pair I see more plainly as I write—the young girl with her soft eyes and her sunny hair, or the old gentleman with the erect though wasted figure, the noble forehead, the steady eye, the parchment skin, the white imperial, and the eternal cigarette between his shrivelled lips.

No need to say that I came more in contact with the young girl. She was not less charming in my eyes because she provoked me greatly as I came to know her intimately. She had many irritating faults. Like most young persons of intellect and inexperience, she was hasty and intolerant in nearly all her judgments, and rather given to being critical in a crude way. She was very musical, playing the guitar and singing in a style that made our shipboard concerts vastly superior to the average of their order; but I have seen her shudder at the efforts of less gifted folks who were also doing their best; and it was the same in other directions where her superiority was less specific. The faults which are most exasperating in another are, of course, one's own faults; and I confess that I was very critical of Eva Denison's criticisms. Then she had a little weakness for exaggeration,

Love on the Ocean

for unconscious egotism in conversation, and I itched to tell her so. I felt so certain that the girl had a fine character underneath, which would rise to noble heights in stress or storm: all the more would I long now to take her in hand and mould her in little things, and anon to take her in my arms just as she was. The latter feeling was resolutely crushed. To be plain, I had endured what is euphemistically called "disappointment" already; and, not being a complete coxcomb, I had no intention of courting a second.

Yet, when I write of Eva Denison, I am like to let my pen outrun my tale. I lay the pen down, and a hundred of her sayings ring in my ears, with my own contradictious comments, that I was doomed so soon to repent; a hundred visions of her start to my eyes; and there is the trade-wind singing in the rigging, and loosening a tress of my darling's hair, till it flies like a tiny golden streamer in the tropic sun. There, it is out! I have called her what she was to be in my heart ever after. Yet at the time I must argue with her—with her! When all my courage should have gone to love-making, I was plucking it up to sail as near as I might to plain remonstrance! I little dreamt how the ghost of every petty word was presently to return and torture me.

Dead Men Tell No Tales

So it is that I can see her and hear her now on a hundred separate occasions—beneath the awning—beneath the stars—on deck—below—at noon or night—but plainest of all in the evening of the day we signalled the Island of Ascension, at the close of that last concert on the quarter-deck. The watch are taking down the extra awning; they are removing the bunting and the footlights. The lanterns are trailed forward before they are put out; from the break of the poop we watch the vivid shifting patch of deck that each lights up on its way. The stars are very sharp in the vast violet dome above our masts; they shimmer on the sea; and our trucks describe minute orbits among the stars, for the trades have yet to fail us, and every inch of canvas has its fill of the gentle steady wind. It is a heavenly night. The peace of God broods upon His waters. No jarring note offends the ear. In the forecastle a voice is humming a song of Eva Denison's that has caught the fancy of the men; the young girl who sang it so sweetly not twenty minutes since— who sang it again and again to please the crew— she alone is at war with our little world—she alone would head a mutiny if she could.

"I *hate* the captain!" she says again.

"My dear Miss Denison!" I begin; for she

has always been severe upon our bluff old man, and it is not the spirit of contrariety alone which makes me invariably take his part. Coarse he may be, and not one whom the owners would have chosen to command the *Lady Jermyn;* a good seaman none the less, who brought us round the Horn in foul weather without losing stitch or stick. I think of the ruddy ruffian in his dripping oilskins, on deck day and night for our sakes, and once more I must needs take his part; but Miss Denison stops me before I can get out another word.

"I am not dear, and I'm not yours," she cries. "I'm only a school-girl—you have all but told me so before to-day! If I were a man—if I were you—I should tell Captain Harris what I thought of him!"

"Why? What has he done now?"

"Now? You know how rude he was to poor Mr. Ready this very afternoon!"

It was true. He had been very rude indeed. But Ready also had been at fault. It may be that I was always inclined to take an opposite view, but I felt bound to point this out, and at any cost.

"You mean when Ready asked him if we were out of our course? I must say I thought it was a silly question to put. It was the same the other evening about the cargo. If the skipper says we're in ballast why not believe him? Why repeat steerage gossip, about mysterious cargoes, at the cuddy table? Captains are always touchy about that sort of thing. I wasn't surprised at his letting out."

My poor love stares at me in the starlight. Her great eyes flash their scorn. Then she gives a little smile—and then a little nod—more scornful than all the rest.

"You never are surprised, are you, Mr. Cole?" says she. "You were not surprised when the wretch used horrible language in front of me! You were not surprised when it was a—dying man—whom he abused!"

I try to soothe her. I agree heartily with her disgust at the epithets employed in her hearing, and towards an invalid, by the irate skipper. But I ask her to make allowances for a rough, uneducated man, rather clumsily touched upon his tender spot. I shall conciliate her presently; the divine pout (so childish it was!) is fading from her lips; the starlight is on the tulle and lace and roses of her pretty evening dress, with its festooned skirts and obsolete flounces; and I am watching her, ay, and worshipping her, though I do not know it yet. And as we stand there comes another snatch from the forecastle:—

Love on the Ocean

"What will you do, love, when I am going,
　　　　With white sail flowing,
　　　　The seas beyond?
　　What will you do, love——"

"They may make the most of that song," says Miss Denison grimly; "it's the last they'll have from me. Get up as many more concerts as you like. I won't sing at another unless it's in the fo'c'sle. I'll sing to the men, but not to Captain Harris. He didn't put in an appearance tonight. He shall not have another chance of insulting me."

Was it her vanity that was wounded after all?

"You forget," said I, "that you would not answer when he addressed you at dinner."

"I should think I wouldn't, after the way he spoke to Mr. Ready; and he too agitated to come to table, poor fellow!"

"Still, the captain felt the open slight."

"Then he shouldn't have used such language in front of me."

"Your father felt it, too, Miss Denison."

I hear nothing plainer than her low but quick reply:

"Mr. Cole, my father has been dead many, many years; he died before I can remember. That man only married my poor mother. He sympa-

thizes with Captain Harris—against me; no
father would do that. Look at them together
now! And you take his side, too; oh! I have
no patience with any of you—except poor Mr.
Ready in his berth."

"But you are not going."

"Indeed I am. I am tired of you all."

And she was gone with angry tears for which
I blamed myself as I fell to pacing the weather
side of the poop—and so often afterwards! So
often, and with such unavailing bitterness!

Senhor Santos and the captain were in conversation by the weather rail. I fancied poor old Harris eyed me with suspicion, and I wished he had
better cause. The Portuguese, however, saluted
me with his customary courtesy, and I thought
there was a grave twinkle in his steady eye.

"Are you in deesgrace also, friend Cole?" he
inquired in his all but perfect English.

"More or less," said I ruefully.

He gave the shrug of his country—that delicate
gesture which is done almost entirely with the
back—a subtlety beyond the power of British
shoulders.

"The senhora is both weelful and pivish," said
he, mixing the two vowels which (with the
aspirate) were his only trouble with our tongue.

Love on the Ocean

"It is great grif to me to see her growing so unlike her sainted mother!"

He sighed, and I saw his delicate fingers forsake the cigarette they were rolling to make the sacred sign upon his breast. He was always smoking one cigarette and making another; as he lit the new one the glow fell upon a strange pin that he wore, a pin with a tiny crucifix inlaid in mosaic. So the religious cast of Senhor Santos was brought twice home to me in the same moment, though, to be sure, I had often been struck by it before. And it depressed me to think that so sweet a child as Eva Denison should have spoken harshly of so good a man as her step-father, simply because he had breadth enough to sympathize with a coarse old salt like Captain Harris.

I turned in, however, and I cannot say the matter kept me awake in the separate state-room which was one luxury of our empty saloon. Alas! I was a heavy sleeper then.

CHAPTER II

THE MYSTERIOUS CARGO

"WAKE up, Cole! The ship's on fire!"

It was young Ready's hollow voice, as cool, however, as though he were telling me I was late for breakfast. I started up and sought him wildly in the darkness.

"You're joking," was my first thought and utterance; for now he was lighting my candle, and blowing out the match with a care that seemed in itself a contradiction.

"I wish I were," he answered. "Listen to that!"

He pointed to my cabin ceiling; it quivered and creaked; and all at once I was as a deaf man healed.

One gets inured to noise at sea, but to this day it passes me how even I could have slept an instant in the abnormal din which I now heard raging above my head. Sea-boots stamped; bare feet pattered; men bawled; women shrieked; shouts of terror drowned the roar of command.

The Mysterious Cargo

"Have we long to last?" I asked, as I leaped for my clothes.

"Long enough for you to dress comfortably. Steady, old man! It's only just been discovered; they may get it under. The panic's the worst part at present, and we're out of that."

But was Eva Denison? Breathlessly I put the question; his answer was reassuring. Miss Denison was with her step-father on the poop. "And both of 'em as cool as cucumbers," added Ready.

They could not have been cooler than this young man, with death at the bottom of his bright and sunken eyes. He was of the type which is all muscle and no constitution; athletes one year, dead men the next; but until this moment the athlete had been to me a mere and incredible tradition. In the afternoon I had seen his lean knees totter under the captain's fire. Now, at midnight —the exact time by my watch—it was as if his shrunken limbs had expanded in his clothes; he seemed hardly to know his own flushed face, as he caught sight of it in my mirror.

"By Jove!" said he, "this has put me in a fine old fever; but I don't know when I felt in better fettle. If only they get it under! I've not looked like this all the voyage."

And he admired himself while I dressed in hot

haste: a fine young fellow; not at all the natural egotist, but cast for death by the doctors, and keenly incredulous in his bag of skin. It revived one's confidence to hear him talk. But he forgot himself in an instant, and gave me a lead through the saloon with a boyish eagerness that made me actually suspicious as I ran. We were nearing the Line. I recalled the excesses of my last crossing, and I prepared for some vast hoax at the last moment. It was only when we plunged upon the crowded quarter-deck, and my own eyes read lust of life and dread of death in the starting eyes of others, that such lust and such dread consumed me in my turn, so that my veins seemed filled with fire and ice.

To be fair to those others, I think that the first wild panic was subsiding even then; at least there was a lull, and even a reaction in the right direction on the part of the males in the second class and steerage. A huge Irishman at their head, they were passing buckets towards the after-hold; the press of people hid the hatchway from us until we gained the poop; but we heard the buckets spitting and a hose-pipe hissing into the flames below; and we saw the column of white vapor rising steadily from their midst.

At the break of the poop stood Captain Harris,

The Mysterious Cargo

his legs planted wide apart, very vigorous, very decisive, very profane. And I must confess that the shocking oaths which had brought us round the Horn inspired a kind of confidence in me now. Besides, even from the poop I could see no flames. But the night was as beautiful as it had been an hour or two back; the stars as brilliant, the breeze even more balmy, the sea even more calm; and we were hove-to already, against the worst.

In this hour of peril the poop was very properly invaded by all classes of passengers, in all manner of incongruous apparel, in all stages of fear, rage, grief and hysteria; as we made our way among this motley nightmare throng, I took Ready by the arm.

"The skipper's a brute," said I, "but he's the right brute in the right place to-night, Ready!"

"I hope he may be," was the reply. "But we *were* off our course this afternoon; and we were off it again during the concert, as sure as we're not on it now."

His tone made me draw him to the rail.

"But how do you know? You didn't have another look, did you?"

"Lots of looks—at the stars. He couldn't keep me from consulting them; and I'm just as certain of it as I'm certain that we've a cargo aboard which we're none of us supposed to know anything about."

The latter piece of gossip was, indeed, all over the ship; but this allusion to it struck me as foolishly irrelevant and frivolous. As to the other matter, I suggested that the officers would have had more to say about it than Ready, if there had been anything in it.

"Officers be damned!" cried our consumptive, with a sound man's vigor. "They're ordinary seamen dressed up; I don't believe they've a second mate's certificate between them, and they're frightened out of their souls."

"Well, anyhow, the skipper isn't that."

"No; he's drunk; he can shout straight, but you should hear him try to speak."

I made my way aft without rejoinder. "Invalid's pessimism," was my private comment. And yet the sick man was whole for the time being; the virile spirit was once more master of the recreant members; and it was with illogical relief that I found those I sought standing almost unconcernedly beside the binnacle.

My little friend was, indeed, pale enough, and her eyes great with dismay; but she stood splendidly calm, in her travelling cloak and bonnet, and with all my soul I hailed the hardihood with which I had rightly credited my love. Yes! I loved her then. It had come home to me at last, and I no longer denied it in my heart. In my innocence and my joy I rather blessed the fire for showing me her true self and my own; and there I stood, loving her openly with my eyes (not to lose another instant), and bursting to tell her so with my lips.

But there also stood Senhor Santos, almost precisely as I had seen him last, cigarette, tie-pin, and all. He wore an overcoat, however, and leaned upon a massive ebony cane, while he carried his daughter's guitar in its case, exactly as though they were waiting for a train. Moreover, I thought that for the first time he was regarding me with no very favoring glance.

"You don't think it serious?" I asked him abruptly, my heart still bounding with the most incongruous joy.

He gave me his ambiguous shrug; and then, "A fire at sea is surely sirrious," said he.

"Where did it break out?"

"No one knows; it may have come of your concert."

"But they are getting the better of it?"

"They are working wonders so far, senhor.

"You see, Miss Denison," I continued ecstatically, "our rough old diamond of a skipper is the right man in the right place after all. A tight man in a tight place, eh?" and I laughed like an idiot in their calm grave faces.

"Senhor Cole is right," said Santos, "although his 'ilarity sims a leetle out of place. But you must never spik against Captain 'Arrees again, menina."

"I never will," the poor child said; yet I saw her wince whenever the captain raised that hoarse voice of his in more and more blasphemous exhortation; and I began to fear with Ready that the man was drunk.

My eyes were still upon my darling, devouring her, revelling in her, when suddenly I saw her hand twitch within her step-father's arm. It was an answering start to one on his part. The cigarette was snatched from his lips. There was a commotion forward, and a cry came aft, from mouth to mouth:

"The flames! The flames!"

I turned, and caught their reflection on the white column of smoke and steam. I ran forward, and saw them curling and leaping in the hell-mouth of the hold.

The quarter-deck now staged a lurid scene: that blazing trap-door in its midst; and each man

The Mysterious Cargo

there a naked demon madly working to save his roasting skin. Abaft the mainmast the deck-pump was being ceaselessly worked by relays of the passengers; dry blankets were passed forward, soaking blankets were passed aft, and flung flat into the furnace one after another. These did more good than the pure water: the pillar of smoke became blacker, denser: we were at a crisis; a sudden hush denoted it; even our hoarse skippr stood dumb.

I had rushed down into the waist of the ship—blushing for my delay—and already I was tossing blankets with the rest. Looking up in an enforced pause, I saw Santos whispering in the skipper's ear, with the expression of a sphinx, but no lack of foreign gesticulation—behind them a fringe of terror-stricken faces, parted at that instant by two more figures, as wild and strange as any in that wild, strange scene. One was our luckless lucky digger, the other a gigantic Zambesi nigger, who for days had been told off to watch him; this was the servant (or rather the slave) of Senhor Santos.

The digger planted himself before the captain. His face was reddened by a fire as consuming as that within the bowels of our gallant ship. He had a huge, unwieldy bundle under either arm.

"Plain question—plain answer," we heard

him stutter. "Is there any — — chance of saving this — — ship?"

His adjectives were too foul for print; they were given with such a special effort at distinctness, however, that I was smiling one instant, and giving thanks the next that Eva Denison had not come forward with her guardian. Meanwhile the skipper had exchanged a glance with Senhor Santos, and I think we all felt that he was going to tell us the truth.

He told it in two words—

"Very little."

Then the first individual tragedy was enacted before every eye. With a yell the drunken maniac rushed to the rail. The nigger was at his heels— he was too late. Uttering another and more piercing shriek, the madman was overboard at a bound; one of his bundles preceded him; the other dropped like a cannon-ball on the deck.

The nigger caught it up and carried it forward to the captain.

Harris held up his hand. We were still before we had fairly found our tongues. His words did run together a little, but he was not drunk.

"Men and women," said he, "what I told that poor devil is Gospel truth; but I didn't tell him we'd no chance of saving our lives, did I? Not

The Mysterious Cargo

me, because we have! Keep your heads and listen to me. There's two good boats on the davits amidships; the chief will take one, the second officer the other; and there ain't no reason why every blessed one of you shouldn't sleep in Ascension to-morrow night. As for me, let me see every soul off of my ship and perhaps I may follow; but by the God that made you, look alive! Mr. Arnott—Mr. McClellan—man them boats and lower away. You can't get quit o' the ship too soon, an' I don't mind tellin' you why. I'll tell you the worst, an' then you'll know. There's been a lot o' gossip goin', gossip about my cargo. I give out as I'd none but ship's stores and ballast, an' I give out a lie. I don't mind tellin' you now. I give out a cussed lie, but I give it out for the good o' the ship! What was the use o' frightenin' folks? But where's the sense in keepin' it back now? We *have* a bit of a cargo," shouted Harris; "and it's gunpowder—every damned ton of it!"

The effect of this announcement may be imagined; my hand has not the cunning to reproduce it on paper; and if it had, it would shrink from the task. Mild men became brutes, brutal men, devils, women—God help them!—shrieking beldams for the most part. Never shall I forget them with their streaming hair, their screaming open mouths, and the cruel ascending fire glinting on their starting eyeballs!

Pell-mell they tumbled down the poop-ladders; pell-mell they raced amidships past that yawning open furnace; the pitch was boiling through the seams of the crackling deck; they slipped and fell upon it, one over another, and the wonder is that none plunged headlong into the flames. A handful remained on the poop, cowering and undone with terror. Upon these turned Captain Harris, as Ready and I, stemming the torrent of maddened humanity, regained the poop ourselves.

"For'ard with ye!" yelled the skipper. "The powder's underneath you in the lazarette!"

They were gone like hunted sheep. And now abaft the flaming hatchway there were only we four surviving saloon passengers, the captain, his steward, the Zambesi negro, and the quartermaster at the wheel. The steward and the black I observed putting stores aboard the captain's gig as it overhung the water from the stern davits.

"Now, gentlemen," said Harris to the two of us, "I must trouble you to step forward with the rest. Senhor Santos insists on taking his chance along with the young lady in my gig. I've told him the risk, but he insists, and the gig'll hold no more."

"But she must have a crew, and I can row. For God's sake take me, captain!" cried I; for Eva Denison sat weeping in her deck chair, and my heart bled faint at the thought of leaving her, I who loved her so, and might die without ever telling her my love! Harris, however, stood firm.

"There's that quartermaster and my steward, and José the nigger," said he. "That's quite enough, Mr. Cole, for I ain't above an oar myself; but, by God, I'm skipper o' this here ship, and I'll skip her as long as I remain aboard!"

I saw his hand go to his belt; I saw the pistols stuck there for mutineers. I looked at Santos. He answered me with his neutral shrug, and, by my soul, he struck a match and lit a cigarette in that hour of life and death! Then last I looked at Ready; and he leant invertebrate over the rail, gasping pitiably from his exertions in regaining the poop, a dying man once more. I pointed out his piteous state.

"At least," I whispered, "you won't refuse to take him?"

"Will there be anything to take?" said the captain brutally.

Dead Men Tell No Tales

Santos advanced leisurely, and puffed his cigarette over the poor wasted and exhausted frame.

"It is for you to decide, captain," said he cynically; "but this one will make no deeference. Yes, I would take him. It will not be far," he added, in a tone that was not the less detestable for being lowered.

"Take them both!" moaned little Eva, putting in her first and last sweet word.

"Then we all drown, Evasinha," said her stepfather. "It is impossible."

"We're too many for her as it is," said the captain. "So for'ard with ye, Mr. Cole, before it's too late."

But my darling's brave word for me had fired my blood, and I turned with equal resolution on Harris and on the Portuguese. "I will go like a lamb," said I, "if you will first give me five minutes' conversation with Miss Denison. Otherwise I do not go; and as for the gig, you may take me or leave me, as you choose."

"What have you to say to her?" asked Santos, coming up to me, and again lowering his voice.

I lowered mine still more. "That I love her!" I answered in a soft ecstasy. "That she may remember how I loved her, if I die!"

His shoulders shrugged a cynical acquiescence.

The Mysterious Cargo

"By all mins, senhor; there is no harm in that."

I was at her side before another word could pass his withered lips.

"Miss Denison, will you grant me five minutes' conversation? It may be the last that we shall ever have together!"

Uncovering her face, she looked at me with a strange terror in her great eyes; then with a questioning light that was yet more strange, for in it there was a wistfulness I could not comprehend. She suffered me to take her hand, however, and to lead her unresisting to the weather rail.

"What is it you have to say?" she asked me in her turn. "What is it that you—think?"

Her voice fell as though she must have the truth.

"That we have all a very good chance," said I heartily.

"Is that all?" cried Eva, and my heart sank at her eager manner.

She seemed at once disappointed and relieved. Could it be possible she dreaded a declaration which she had foreseen all along? My evil first experience rose up to warn me. No, I would not speak now; it was no time. If she loved me, it might make her love me less; better to trust to God to spare us both.

Dead Men Tell No Tales

"Yes, it is all," I said doggedly.

She drew a little nearer, hesitating. It was as though her disappointment had gained on her relief.

"Do you know what I thought you were going to say?"

"No, indeed."

"Dare I tell you?"

"You can trust me."

Her pale lips parted. Her great eyes shone. Another instant, and she had told me that which I would have given all but life itself to know. But in that tick of time a quick step came behind me, and the light went out of the sweet face upturned to mine.

"I cannot! I must not! Here is—that man!"

Senhor Santos was all smiles and rings of pale-blue smoke.

"You will be cut off, friend Cole," said he. "The fire is spreading."

"Let it spread!" I cried, gazing my very soul into the young girl's eyes. "We have not finished our conversation."

"We have!" said she, with sudden decision. "Go—go—for my sake—for your own sake—go at once!"

She gave me her hand. I merely clasped it.

The Mysterious Cargo

And so I left her at the rail—ah, heaven! how often we had argued on that very spot! So I left her, with the greatest effort of all my life (but one); and yet in passing, full as my heart was of love and self, I could not but lay a hand on poor Ready's shoulders.

"God bless you, old boy!" I said to him.

He turned a white face that gave me half an instant's pause.

"It's all over with me this time," he said. "But, I say, I was right about the cargo?"

And I heard a chuckle as I reached the ladder; but Ready was no longer in my mind; even Eva was driven out of it, as I stood aghast on the topmost rung.

CHAPTER III

TO THE WATER'S EDGE

IT was not the new panic amidships that froze my marrow; it was not that the pinnace hung perpendicularly by the fore-tackle, and had shot out those who had swarmed aboard her before she was lowered, as a cart shoots a load of bricks. It was bad enough to see the whole boat-load struggling, floundering, sinking in the sea; for selfish eyes (and which of us is all unselfish at such a time?) there was a worse sight yet; for I saw all this across an impassable gulf of fire.

The quarter-deck had caught: it was in flames to port and starboard of the flaming hatch; only fore and aft of it was the deck sound to the lips of that hideous mouth, with the hundred tongues shooting out and up.

Could I jump it there? I sprang down and looked. It was only a few feet across; but to leap through that living fire was to leap into eternity. I drew back instantly, less because my heart failed me, I may truly say, than because my common sense did not.

To the Water's Edge

Some were watching me, it seemed, across this hell. "The bulwarks!" they screamed. "Walk along the bulwarks!" I held up my hand in token that I heard and understood and meant to act. And as I did their bidding I noticed what indeed had long been apparent to idler eyes: the wind was not; we had lost our southeast trades; the doomed ship was rolling in a dead calm.

Rolling, rolling, rolling so that it seemed minutes before I dared to move an inch. Then I tried it on my hands and knees, but the scorched bulwarks burned me to the bone. And then I leapt up, desperate with the pain; and, with my tortured hands spread wide to balance me, I walked those few yards, between rising sea and falling fire, and falling sea and rising fire, as an acrobat walks a rope, and by God's grace without mishap.

There was no time to think twice about my feat, or, indeed, about anything else that befell upon a night when each moment was more pregnant than the last. And yet I did think that those who had encouraged me to attempt so perilous a trick might have welcomed me alive among them; they were looking at something else already; and this was what it was.

One of the cabin stewards had presented himself on the poop; he had a bottle in one hand, a

Dead Men Tell No Tales

glass in the other; in the red glare we saw him dancing in front of the captain like an unruly marionette. Harris appeared to threaten him. What he said we could not hear for the deep-drawn blast and the high staccato crackle of the blazing hold. But we saw the staggering steward offering him a drink; saw the glass flung next instant in the captain's face, the blood running, a pistol drawn, fired without effect, and snatched away by the drunken mutineer. Next instant a smooth black cane was raining blow after blow on the man's head. He dropped; the blows fell thick and heavy as before. He lay wriggling; the Portuguese struck and struck until he lay quite still; then we saw Joaquin Santos kneel, and rub his stick carefully on the still thing's clothes, as a man might wipe his boots.

Curses burst from our throats; yet the fellow deserved to die. Nor, as I say, had we time to waste two thoughts upon any one incident. This last had begun and ended in the same minute; in another we were at the starboard gangway, tumbling helter-skelter aboard the lowered long-boat.

She lay safely on the water: how we thanked our gods for that! Lower and lower sank her gunwale as we dropped aboard her, with no more care than the Gadarene swine whose fate we

To the Water's Edge

courted. Discipline, order, method, common care, we brought none of these things with us from our floating furnace; but we fought to be first over the bulwarks, and in the bottom of the long-boat we fought again.

And yet she held us all! All, that is, but a terror-stricken few, who lay along the jibboom like flies upon a stick: all but two or three more whom we left fatally hesitating in the forechains: all but the selfish savages who had been the first to perish in the pinnace, and one distracted couple who had thrown their children into the kindly ocean, and jumped in after them out of their torment, locked for ever in each other's arms.

Yes! I saw more things on that starry night, by that blood-red glare, than I have told you in their order, and more things than I shall tell you now. Blind would I gladly be for my few remaining years, if that night's horrors could be washed from these eyes for ever. I have said so much, however, that in common candor I must say one thing more. I have spoken of selfish savages. God help me and forgive me! For by this time I was one myself.

In the long-boat we cannot have been less than thirty; the exact number no man will ever know. But we shoved off without mischance; the chief

Dead Men Tell No Tales

mate had the tiller; the third mate the boat-hook; and six or eight oars were at work, in a fashion, as we plunged among the great smooth sickening mounds and valleys of fathomless ink.

Scarcely were we clear when the foremast dropped down on the fastenings, dashing the jib-boom into the water with its load of demented human beings. The mainmast followed by the board before we had doubled our distance from the wreck. Both trailed to port, where we could not see them; and now the mizzen stood alone in sad and solitary grandeur, her flapping idle sails lighted up by the spreading conflagration, so that they were stamped very sharply upon the black and starry sky. But the whole scene from the long-boat was one of startling brilliancy and horror. The fire now filled the entire waist of the vessel, and the noise of it was as the rumble and roar of a volcano. As for the light, I declare that it put many a star clean out, and dimmed the radiance of all the rest, as it flooded the sea for miles around, and a sea of molten glass reflected it. My gorge rose at the long, low billows—sleek as black satin—lifting and dipping in this ghastly glare. I preferred to keep my eyes upon the little ship burning like a tar barrel as the picture grew. But presently I thanked God aloud: there was the

34

gig swimming like a beetle over the bloodshot rollers in our wake.

In our unspeakable gladness at being quit of the ship, some minutes passed before we discovered that the long-boat was slowly filling. The water was at our ankles before a man of us cried out, so fast were our eyes to the poor lost *Lady Jermyn*. Then all at once the ghastly fact dawned upon us; and I think it was the mate himself who burst out crying like a child. I never ascertained, however, for I had kicked off my shoes and was busy baling with them. Others were hunting for the leak. But the mischief was as subtle as it was mortal—as though a plank had started from end to end. Within and without the waters rose equally—then lay an instant level with our gunwales—then swamped us, oh! so slowly, that I thought we were never going to sink. It was like getting inch by inch into your tub; I can feel it now, creeping, crawling up my back. "It's coming! O Christ!" muttered one as it came; to me it was a downright relief to be carried under at last.

But then, thank God, I have always been a strong swimmer. The water was warm and buoyant, and I came up like a cork, as I knew I should. I shook the drops from my face, and

Dead Men Tell No Tales

there were the sweet stars once more; for many an eye they had gone out for ever; and there the burning wreck.

A man floundered near me, in a splutter of phosphorescence. I tried to help him, and in an instant he had me wildly round the neck. In the end I shook him off, poor devil, to his death. And he was the last I tried to aid: have I not said already what I was become?

In a little an oar floated my way: I threw my arms across it and gripped it with my chin as I swam. It relieved me greatly. Up and down I rode among the oily black hillocks; I was down when there was a sudden flare as though the sun had risen, and I saw still a few heads bobbing and a few arms waving frantically around me. At the same instant a terrific detonation split the ears; and when I rose on the next bald billow, where the ship lay burning a few seconds before, there remained but a red-hot spine that hissed and dwindled for another minute, and then left a blackness through which every star shone with redoubled brilliance.

And now right and left splashed falling missiles; a new source of danger or of temporary respite; to me, by a merciful Providence, it proved the latter.

To the Water's Edge

Some heavy thing fell with a mighty splash right in front of me. A few more yards, and my brains had floated with the spume. As it was, the oar was dashed from under my armpits; in another moment they had found a more solid resting-place.

It was a hen-coop, and it floated bars upwards like a boat. In this calm it might float for days. I climbed upon the bars—and the whole cage rolled over on top of me.

Coming to the surface, I found to my joy that the hen-coop had righted itself; so now I climbed up again, but this time very slowly and gingerly; the balance was undisturbed, and I stretched myself cautiously along the bars on my stomach. A good idea immediately occurred to me. I had jumped as a matter of course into the flannels which one naturally wears in the tropics. To their lightness I already owed my life, but the common cricket-belt which was part of the costume was the thing to which I owe it most of all. Loosening this belt a little, as I tucked my toes tenaciously under the endmost bar, I undid and passed the two ends under one of the middle bars, fastening the clasp upon the other side. If I capsized now, well, we might go to the bottom together; otherwise the hen-coop and I should not part company

Dead Men Tell No Tales

in a hurry; and I thought, I felt, that she would float.

Worn out as I was, and comparatively secure for the moment, I will not say that I slept; but my eyes closed, and every fibre rested, as I rose and slid with the smooth, long swell. Whether I did indeed hear voices, curses, cries, I cannot say positively to this day. I only know that I raised my head and looked sharply all ways but the way I durst not look for fear of an upset. And, again, I thought I saw first a tiny flame, and then a tinier glow; and as my head drooped, and my eyes closed again, I say I *thought* I smelt tobacco; but this, of course, was my imagination supplying all the links from one.

CHAPTER IV.

THE SILENT SEA

REMEMBER (if indeed there be any need to remind you) that it is a flagrant landsman who is telling you this tale. Nothing know I of seamanship, save what one could not avoid picking up on the round voyage of the *Lady Jermyn,* never to be completed on this globe. I may be told that I have burned that devoted vessel as nothing ever burned on land or sea. I answer that I write of what I saw, and that is not altered by a miscalled spar or a misunderstood manœuvre. But now I am aboard a craft I handle for myself, and must make shift to handle a second time with this frail pen.

The hen-coop was some six feet long, by eighteen or twenty inches in breadth and depth. It was simply a long box with bars in lieu of a lid; but it was very strongly built.

I recognized it as one of two which had stood lashed against either rail of the *Lady Jermyn's* poop; there the bars had risen at right angles to the deck; now they lay horizontal, a gridiron six feet long—and my bed. And as each particular bar left its own stripe across my wearied body, and yet its own comfort in my quivering heart, another day broke over the face of the waters, and over me.

Discipline, what there was of it originally, had been the very first thing to perish aboard our ill-starred ship; the officers, I am afraid, were not much better than poor Ready made them out (thanks to Bendigo and Ballarat), and little had been done in true ship-shape style all night. All hands had taken their spell at everything as the fancy seized them; not a bell had been struck from first to last; and I can only conjecture that the fire raged four or five hours, from the fact that it was midnight by my watch when I left it on my cabin drawers, and that the final extinction of the smouldering keel was so soon followed by the first deep hint of dawn. The rest took place with the trite rapidity of the equatorial latitudes. It had been my foolish way to pooh-pooh the old saying that there is no twilight in the tropics. I saw more truth in it as I lay lonely on this heaving waste.

The stars were out; the sea was silver; the sun was up.

And oh! the awful glory of that sunrise! It

The Silent Sea

was terrific; it was sickening; my senses swam. Sunlit billows smooth and sinister, without a crest, without a sound; miles and miles of them as I rose; an oily grave among them as I fell. Hill after hill of horror, valley after valley of despair! The face of the waters in petty but eternal unrest; and now the sun must shine to set it smiling, to show me its cruel ceaseless mouthings, to reveal all but the ghastlier horrors underneath.

How deep was it? I fell to wondering! Not that it makes any difference whether you drown in one fathom or in ten thousand, whether you fall from a balloon or from the attic window. But the greater depth or distance is the worse to contemplate; and I was as a man hanging by his hands so high above the world, that his dangling feet cover countries, continents; a man who must fall very soon, and wonders how long he will be falling, falling; and how far his soul will bear his body company.

In time I became more accustomed to the sun upon this heaving void; less frightened, as a child is frightened, by the mere picture. And I have still the impression that, as hour followed hour since the falling of the wind, the nauseous swell in part subsided. I seemed less often on an eminence or in a pit; my glassy azure dales had gentler slopes, or a distemper was melting from my eyes.

At least I know that I had now less work to keep my frail ship trim, though this also may have come by use and practice. In the beginning one or other of my legs had been for ever trailing in the sea, to keep the hen-coop from rolling over the other way; in fact, as I understand they steer the toboggan in Canada, so I my little bark. Now the necessity for this was gradually decreasing; whatever the cause, it was the greatest mercy the day had brought me yet. With less strain on the attention, however, there was more upon the mind. No longer forced to exert some muscle twice or thrice a minute, I had time to feel very faint, and yet time to think. My soul flew homing to its proper prison. I was no longer any unit at unequal strife with the elements; instincts common to my kind were no longer my only stimulus. I was my poor self again; it was my own little life, and no other, that I wanted to go on living; and yet I felt vaguely there was some special thing I wished to live for, something that had not been very long in my ken; something that had perhaps nerved and strengthened me all these hours. What, then, could it be?

I could not think. For moments or for min-

The Silent Sea

utes I wondered stupidly, dazed as I was. Then I remembered—and the tears gushed to my eyes. How could I ever have forgotten? I deserved it all, all, all! To think that many a time we must have sat together on this very coop! I kissed its blistering edge at the thought, and my tears ran afresh, as though they never would stop.

Ah! how I thought of her as that cruel day's most cruel sun climbed higher and higher in the flawless flaming vault. A pocket-handkerchief of all things had remained in my trousers pocket through fire and water; I knotted it on the old childish plan, and kept it ever drenched upon the head that had its own fever to endure as well. Eva Denison! Eva Denison! I was talking to her in the past, I was talking to her in the future, and oh! how different were the words, the tone! Yes, I hated myself for having forgotten her; but I hated God for having given her back to my tortured brain; it made life so many thousand-fold more sweet, and death so many thousandfold more bitter.

She was saved in the gig. Sweet Jesus, thanks for that! But I—I was dying a lingering death in mid-ocean; she would never know how I loved her, I, who could only lecture her when I had her at my side.

43

Dead Men Tell No Tales

Dying? No—no—not yet! I must live—live —live—to tell my darling how I had loved her all the time. So I forced myself from my lethargy of despair and grief; and this thought, the sweetest thought of all my life, may or may not have been my unrealized stimulus ere now; it was in very deed my most conscious and perpetual spur henceforth until the end.

From this onward, while my sense stood by me, I was practical, resourceful, alert. It was now high-noon, and I had eaten nothing since dinner the night before. How clearly I saw the long saloon table, only laid, however, abaft the mast; the glittering glass, the cool white napery, the poor old dried dessert in the green dishes! Earlier, this had occupied my mind an hour; now I dismissed it in a moment; there was Eva, I must live for her; there must be ways of living at least a day or two without sustenance, and I must think of them.

So I undid that belt of mine which fastened me to my gridiron, and I straddled my craft with a sudden keen eye for sharks, of which I never once had thought until now. Then I tightened the belt about my hollow body, and just sat there with the problem. The past hour I had been wholly unobservant; the inner eye had had its turn; but

The Silent Sea

that was over now, and I sat as upright as possible, seeking greedily for a sail. Of course I saw none. Had we indeed been off our course before the fire broke out? Had we burned to cinders aside and apart from the regular track of ships? Then, though my present valiant mood might ignore the adverse chances, they were as one hundred to a single chance of deliverance. Our burning had brought no ship to our succor; and how should I, a mere speck amid the waves, bring one to mine?

Moreover, I was all but motionless; I was barely drifting at all. This I saw from a few objects which were floating around me now at noon; they had been with me when the high sun rose. One was, I think, the very oar which had been my first support; another was a sailor's cap; but another, which floated nearer, was new to me, as though it had come to the surface while my eyes were turned inwards. And this was clearly the case; for the thing was a drowned and bloated corpse.

It fascinated me, though not with extraordinary horror; it came too late to do that. I thought I recognized the man's back. I fancied it was the mate who had taken charge of the long-boat. Was I then the single survivor of those thirty

souls? I was still watching my poor lost comrade, when that happened to him against which
even I was not proof. Through the deep translu-
cent blue beneath me a slim shape glided; three
smaller fish led the way; they dallied an instant
a fathom under my feet, which were snatched up,
with what haste you may imagine; then on they
went to surer prey.

He turned over; his dreadful face stared upwards; it was the chief officer, sure enough. Then
he clove the water with a rush, his dead hand
waved, the last of him to disappear; and I had
a new horror to think over for my sins. His
poor fingers were all broken and beaten to a
pulp.

The voices of the night came back to me—the
curses and the cries. Yes, I must have heard
them. In memory now I recognized the voice
of the chief mate, but there again came in the
assisted imagination. Yet I was not so sure of
this as before. I thought of Santos and his horrible heavy cane. Good God! she was in the power
of *that!* I must live for Eva indeed; must save
myself to save and protect my innocent and helpless girl.

Again I was a man; stronger than ever was the
stimulus now, louder than ever the call on every

The Silent Sea

drop of true man's blood in my perishing frame. It should not perish! It should not!

Yet my throat was parched; my lips were caked; my frame was hollow. Very weak I was already; without sustenance I should surely die. But as yet I was far enough from death, or I had done disdaining the means of life that all this time lay ready to my hand. A number of dead fowls imparted ballast to my little craft.

Yet I could not look at them in all these hours; or I could look, but that was all. So I must sit up one hour more, and keep a sharper eye than ever for the tiniest glimmer of a sail. To what end, I often asked myself? I might see them; they would never see me.

Then my eyes would fall, and "you squeamish fool!" I said at intervals, until my tongue failed to articulate; it had swollen so in my mouth. Flying fish skimmed the water like thick spray; petrels were so few that I could count them; another shark swam round me for an hour. In sudden panic I dashed my knuckles on the wooden bars, to get at a duck to give the monster for a sop. My knuckles bled. I held them to my mouth. My cleaving tongue wanted more. The duck went to the shark; a few minutes more and I had made my own vile meal as well.

47

CHAPTER V

MY REWARD

THE sun declined; my shadow broadened on the waters; and now I felt that if my cockle-shell could live a little longer, why, so could I.

I had got at the fowls without further hurt. Some of the bars took out, I discovered how. And now very carefully I got my legs in, and knelt; but the change of posture was not worth the risk one ran for it; there was too much danger of capsizing, and failing to free oneself before she filled and sank.

With much caution I began breaking the bars, one by one; it was hard enough, weak as I was; my thighs were of more service than my hands.

But at last I could sit, the grating only covering me from the knees downwards. And the relief of that outweighed all the danger, which, as I discovered to my untold joy, was now much less than it had been before.

I was better ballast than the fowls.

These I had attached to the lashings which had been blown asunder by the explosion; at one end of the coop the ring-bolt had been torn clean out,

My Reward

but at the other it was the cordage that had parted. To the frayed ends I tied my fowls by the legs, with the most foolish pride in my own cunning. Do you not see? It would keep them fresh for my use, and it was a trick I had read of in no book; it was all my own.

So evening fell and found me hopeful and even puffed up; but yet, no sail.

Now, however, I could lie back, and use had given me a strange sense of safety; besides, I think I knew, I hope I felt, that the hen-coop was in other Hands than mine.

All is reaction in the heart of man; light follows darkness nowhere more surely than in that hidden self, and now at sunset it was my heart's high-noon. Deep peace pervaded me as I lay outstretched in my narrow rocking bed, as it might be in my coffin; a trust in my Maker's will to save me if that were for the best, a trust in His final wisdom and loving-kindness, even though this night should be my last on earth. For myself I was resigned, and for others I must trust Him no less. Who was I to constitute myself the protector of the helpless, when He was in His Heaven? Such was my sunset mood; it lasted a few minutes, and then, without radically changing, it became more objective.

Dead Men Tell No Tales

The west was a broadening blaze of yellow and purple and red. I cannot describe it to you. If you have seen the sun set in the tropics, you would despise my description; and, if not, I for one could never make you see it. Suffice it that a petrel wheeled somewhere between deepening carmine and paling blue, and it took my thoughts off at an earthy tangent. I thanked God there were no big sea-birds in these latitudes; no molly-hawks, no albatrosses, no Cape-hens. I thought of an albatross that I had caught going out. Its beak and talons were at the bottom with the charred remains of the *Lady Jermyn*. But I could see them still, could feel them shrewdly in my mind's flesh; and so to the old superstition, strangely justified by my case; and so to the poem which I, with my special experience, not unnaturally consider the greatest poem ever penned.

But I did not know it then as I do now—and how the lines eluded me! I seemed to see them in the book, yet I could not read the words!

> "Water, water, everywhere,
> Nor any drop to drink."

That, of course, came first (incorrectly); and it reminded me of my thirst, which the blood of

My Reward

the fowls had so very partially appeased. I see now that it is lucky I could recall but little more. Experience is less terrible than realization, and that poem makes me realize what I went through as memory cannot. It has verses which would have driven me mad. On the other hand, the exhaustive mental search for them distracted my thoughts until the stars were back in the sky; and now I had a new occupation, saying to myself all the poetry I could remember, especially that of the sea; for I was a bookish fellow even then. But I never was anything of a scholar. It is odd, therefore, that the one apposite passage which recurred to me in its entirety was in hexameters and pentameters:—

> Me miserum, quanti montes volvuntur aquarum!
> Jam jam tacturos sidera summa putes.
> Quantæ diducto subsidunt æquore valles!
> Jam jam tacturas Tartara nigra putes.
> Quocunque adspicio, nihil est nisi pontus et æther;
> Fluctibus hic tumidis, nubibus ille minax. . . .

More there was of it in my head; but this much was an accurate statement of my case; and yet less so now (I was thankful to reflect) than in the morning, when every wave was indeed a mountain, and its trough a Tartarus. I had learnt

51

Dead Men Tell No Tales

the lines at school; nay, they had formed my very earliest piece of Latin repetition. And how sharply I saw the room I said them in, the man I said them to, ever since my friend! I figured him even now hearing Ovid rep., the same passage in the same room. And I lay saying it on a hen-coop in the middle of the Atlantic Ocean!

At last I fell into a deep sleep, a long unconscious holiday of the soul, undefiled by any dream. They say that our dreaming is done as we slowly wake; then was I out of the way of it that night, for a sudden violent rocking awoke me in one horrid instant. I made it worse by the way I started to a sitting posture. I had shipped some water. I was shipping more. Yet all around the sea was glassy; whence then the commotion? As my ship came trim again, and I saw that my hour was not yet, the cause occurred to me; and my heart turned so sick that it was minutes before I had the courage to test my theory.

It was the true one.

A shark had been at my trailing fowls; had taken the bunch of them together, dragging the legs from my loose fastenings. Lucky they had been no stronger! Else had I been dragged down to perdition too.

Lucky, did I say? The refinement of cruelty

My Reward

rather; for now I had neither meat nor drink; my throat was a kiln; my tongue a flame; and another day at hand.

The stars were out; the sea was silver; the sun was up!

.   .   .   .   .

Hours passed.

I was waiting now for my delirium.

It came in bits.

I was a child. I was playing on the lawn at home. I was back on the blazing sea.

I was a schoolboy saying my Ovid; then back once more.

The hen-coop was the *Lady Jermyn*. I was at Eva Denison's side. They were marrying us on board. The ship's bell was ringing for us; a guitar in the background burlesqued the Wedding March under skinny fingers; the air was poisoned by a million cigarettes, they raised a pall of smoke above the mastheads, they set fire to the ship; smoke and flame covered the sea from rim to rim, smoke and flame filled the universe; the sea dried up, and I was left lying in its bed, lying in my coffin, with red-hot teeth, because the sun blazed right above them, and my withered lips were drawn back from them for ever.

So once more I came back to my living death;

too weak now to carry a finger to the salt water
and back to my mouth; too weak to think of Eva;
too weak to pray any longer for the end, to trouble
or to care any more.

Only so tired.

.   .   .   .   .

Death has no more terrors for me. I have
supped the last horror of the worst death a man
can die. You shall hear now for what I was de-
livered; you shall read of my reward.

My floating coffin was many things in turn; a
railway carriage, a pleasure boat on the Thames,
a hammock under the trees; last of all it was the
upper berth in a not very sweet-smelling cabin,
with a clatter of knives and forks near at hand,
and a very strong odor of onions in the Irish stew.

My hand crawled to my head; both felt a won-
drous weight; and my head was covered with
bristles no longer than those on my chin, only less
stubborn.

"Where am I?" I feebly asked.

The knives and forks clattered on, and presently
I burst out crying because they had not heard me,
and I knew that I could never make them hear.
Well, they heard my sobs, and a huge fellow came
with his mouth full, and smelling like a pickle
bottle.

My Reward

"Where am I?"

"Aboard the brig *Eliza,* Liverpool, homeward bound; glad to see them eyes open."

"Have I been here long?"

"Matter o' ten days."

"Where did you find me?"

"Floating in a hen-coop; thought you was a dead 'un."

"Do you know what ship?"

"Do we know? No, that's what you've got to tell us!"

"I can't," I sighed, too weak to wag my head upon the pillow.

The man went to my cabin door.

"Here's a go," said he; "forgotten the name of his blessed ship, he has. Where's that there paper, Mr. Bowles? There's just a chance it may be the same."

"I've got it, sir."

"Well, fetch it along, and come you in, Mr. Bowles; likely you may think o' somethin'."

A reddish, hook-nosed man, with a jaunty, wicked look, came and smiled upon me in the friendliest fashion; the smell of onions became more than I knew how to endure.

"Ever hear of the ship *Lady Jermyn?*" asked the first comer, winking at the other.

Dead Men Tell No Tales

I thought very hard, the name did sound familiar; but no, I could not honestly say that I had heard it before.

The captain looked at his mate.

"It was a thousand to one," said he; "still we may as well try him with the other names. Ever heard of Cap'n Harris, mister?"

"Not that I know of."

"Of Saunderson—stooard?"

"No."

"Or Crookes—quartermaster."

"Never."

"Nor yet of Ready—a passenger?"

"No."

"It's no use goin' on," said the captain, folding up the paper.

"None whatever, sir," said the mate.

"Ready! Ready!" I repeated. "I do seem to have heard that name before. Won't you give me another chance?"

The paper was unfolded with a shrug.

"There was another passenger of the name of San—Santos. Dutchman, seemin'ly. Ever heard o' *him?*"

My disappointment was keen. I could not say that I had. Yet I would not swear that I had not.

My Reward

"Oh, won't you? Well, there's only one more chance. Ever heard of Miss Eva Denison——"

"By God, yes! *Have you?*"

I was sitting bolt upright in my bunk. The skipper's beard dropped upon his chest.

"Bless my soul! The last name o' the lot, too!"

"Have *you* heard of her?" I reiterated.

"Wait a bit, my lad! Not so fast. Lie down again and tell me who she was."

"Who she was?" I screamed. "I want to know where she is!"

"I can't hardly say," said the captain awkwardly. "We found the gig o' the *Lady Jermyn* the week arter we found you, bein' becalmed like; there wasn't no lady aboard her, though."

"Was there anybody?"

"Two dead 'uns—an' this here paper."

"Let me see it!"

The skipper hesitated.

"Hadn't you better wait a bit?"

"No, no; for Christ's sake let me see the worst; do you think I can't read it in your face?"

I could—I did. I made that plain to them, and at last I had the paper smoothed out upon my knees. It was a short statement of the last sufferings of those who had escaped in the gig, and there was nothing in it that I did not now expect.

57

Dead Men Tell No Tales

They had buried Ready first—then my darling—then her step-father. The rest expected to follow fast enough. It was all written plainly, on a sheet of the log-book, in different trembling hands. Captain Harris had gone next; and two had been discovered dead.

How long I studied that bit of crumpled paper, with the salt spray still sparkling on it faintly, God alone knows. All at once a peal of nightmare laughter rattled through the cabin. My deliverers atarted back. The laugh was mine.

CHAPTER VI

THE SOLE SURVIVOR

A FEW weeks later I landed in England, I, who no longer desired to set foot on any land again.

At nine-and-twenty I was gaunt and gray; my nerves were shattered, my heart was broken; and my face showed it without let or hindrance from the spirit that was broken too. Pride, will, courage, and endurance, all these had expired in my long and lonely battle with the sea. They had kept me alive—for this. And now they left me naked to mine enemies.

For every hand seemed raised against me, though in reality it was the hand of fellowship that the world stretched out, and the other was the reading of a jaundiced eye. I could not help it: there was a poison in my veins that made me all ingratitude and perversity. The world welcomed me back, and I returned the compliment by sulking like the recaptured runaway I was at heart. The world showed a sudden interest in me; so I took no further interest in the world, but, on the contrary, resented its attentions with unreasonable warmth and obduracy; and my would-be friends I regarded as my very worst enemies. The majority, I feel sure, meant but well and kindly by the poor survivor. But the survivor could not forget that his name was still in the newspapers, nor blink the fact that he was an unworthy hero of the passing hour. And he suffered enough from brazenly meddlesome and self-seeking folk, from impudent and inquisitive intruders, to justify some suspicion of old acquaintances suddenly styling themselves old friends, and of distant connections newly and unduly eager to claim relationship. Many I misjudged, and have long known it. On the whole, however, I wonder at that attitude of mine as little as I approve of it.

If I had distinguished myself in any other way, it would have been a different thing. It was the fussy, sentimental, inconsiderate interest in one thrown into purely accidental and necessarily painful prominence—the vulgarization of an unspeakable tragedy—that my soul abhorred. I confess that I regarded it from my own unique and selfish point of view. What was a thrilling matter to the world was a torturing memory to me. The quintessence of the torture was, moreover, my

The Sole Survivor

own secret. It was not the loss of the *Lady Jermyn* that I could not bear to speak about; it was my own loss; but the one involved the other. My loss apart, however, it was plain enough to dwell upon experiences so terrible and yet so recent as those which I had lived to tell. I did what I considered my duty to the public, but I certainly did no more. My reticence was rebuked in the papers that made the most of me, but would fain have made more. And yet I do not think that I was anything but docile with those who had a manifest right to question me; to the owners, and to other interested persons, with whom I was confronted on one pretext or another, I told my tale as fully and as freely as I have told it here, though each telling hurt more than the last. That was necessary and unavoidable; it was the private intrusions which I resented with all the spleen the sea had left me in exchange for the qualities it had taken away.

Relatives I had as few as misanthropist could desire; but from self-congratulation on the fact, on first landing, I soon came to keen regret. They at least would have sheltered me from spies and busybodies; they at least would have secured the peace and privacy of one who was no hero in fact or spirit, whose noblest deed was a piece of self-

Dead Men Tell No Tales

preservation which he wished undone with all his heart.

Self-consciousness no doubt multiplied my flattering assailants. I have said that my nerves were shattered. I may have imagined much and exaggerated the rest. Yet what truth there was in my suspicions you shall duly see. I felt sure that I was followed in the street, and my every movement dogged by those to whom I would not condescend to turn and look. Meanwhile, I had not the courage to go near my club, and the Temple was a place where I was accosted in every court, effusively congratulated on the marvellous preservation of my stale spoilt life, and invited right and left to spin my yarn over a quiet pipe! Well, perhaps such invitations were not so common as they have grown in my memory; nor must you confuse my then feelings on all these matters with those which I entertain as I write. I have grown older, and, I hope, something kindlier and wiser since then. Yet to this day I cannot blame myself for abandoning my chambers and avoiding my club.

For a temporary asylum I pitched upon a small, quiet, empty, private hotel which I knew of in Charterhouse Square. Instantly the room next mine became occupied.

All the first night I imagined I heard voices talk-

The Sole Survivor

ing about me in that room next door. It was becoming a disease with me. Either I was being dogged, watched, followed, day and night, indoors and out, or I was the victim of a very ominous hallucination. That night I never closed an eye nor lowered my light. In the morning I took a four-wheel cab and drove straight to Harley Street; and, upon my soul, as I stood on the specialist's door-step, I could have sworn I saw the occupant of the room next mine dash by me in a hansom!

"Ah!" said the specialist; "so you cannot sleep; you hear voices; you fancy you are being followed in the street. You don't think these fancies spring entirely from the imagination? Not entirely—just so. And you keep looking behind you, as though somebody were at your elbow; and you prefer to sit with your back close to the wall. Just so—just so. Distressing symptoms, to be sure, but—but hardly to be wondered at in a man who has come through your nervous strain." A keen professional light glittered in his eyes. "And almost commonplace," he added, smiling, "compared with the hallucinations you must have suffered from on that hen-coop! Ah, my dear sir, the psychological interest of your case is very great!"

Dead Men Tell No Tales

"It may be," said I, brusquely. "But I come to you to get that hen-coop out of my head, not to be reminded of it. Everybody asks me about the damned thing, and you follow everybody else. I wish it and I were at the bottom of the sea together!"

This speech had the effect of really interesting the doctor in my present condition, which was indeed one of chronic irritation and extreme excitability, alternating with fits of the very blackest despair. Instead of offending my gentleman I had put him on his mettle, and for half an hour he honored me with the most exhaustive inquisition ever elicited from a medical man. His panacea was somewhat in the nature of an anti-climax, but at least it had the merits of simplicity and of common sense. A change of air—perfect quiet—say a cottage in the country—not too near the sea. And he shook my hand kindly when I left.

"Keep up your heart, my dear sir," said he. "Keep up your courage and your heart."

"My heart!" I cried. "It's at the bottom of the Atlantic Ocean."

He was the first to whom I had said as much. He was a stranger. What did it matter? And, oh, it was so true—so true.

Every day and all day I was thinking of my love;

every hour and all hours she was before me with her sunny hair and young, young face. Her wistful eyes were gazing into mine continually. Their wistfulness I had never realized at the time; but now I did; and I saw it for what it seemed always to have been, the soft, sad, yearning look of one fated to die young. So young—so young! And I might live to be an old man, mourning her.

That I should never love again I knew full well. This time there was no mistake. I have implied, I believe, that it was for another woman I fled originally to the diggings. Well, that one was still unmarried, and when the papers were full of me she wrote me a letter which I now believe to have been merely kind. At the time I was all uncharitableness; but words of mine would fail to tell you how cold this letter left me; it was as a candle lighted in the full blaze of the sun.

With all my bitterness, however, you must not suppose that I had quite lost the feelings which had inspired me at sunset on the lonely ocean, while my mind still held good. I had been too near my Maker ever to lose those feelings altogether. They were with me in the better moments of these my worst days. I trusted His wisdom still. There was a reason for everything; there were reasons for all this. I alone had been saved out of all those

Dead Men Tell No Tales

souls who sailed from Melbourne in the *Lady Jermyn*. Why should I have been the favored one; I with my broken heart and now lonely life? Some great inscrutable reason there must be; at my worst I did not deny that. But neither did I puzzle my sick brain with the reason. I just waited for it to be revealed to me, if it were God's will ever to reveal it. And that I conceive to be the one spirit in which a man may contemplate, with equal sanity and reverence, the mysteries and the miseries of his life.

CHAPTER VII

I FIND A FRIEND

THE night after I consulted the specialist I was quite determined to sleep. I had laid in a bundle of the daily papers. No country cottage was advertised to let but I knew of it by evening, and about all the likely ones I had already written. The scheme occupied my thoughts. Trout-fishing was a desideratum. I would take my rod and plenty of books, would live simply and frugally, and it should make a new man of me by Christmas. It was now October. I went to sleep thinking of autumn tints against an autumn sunset. It must have been very early, certainly not later than ten o'clock; the previous night I had not slept at all.

Now, this private hotel of mine was a very old-fashioned house, dark and dingy all day long, with heavy old chandeliers and black old oak, and dead flowers in broken flower-pots surrounding a grimy grass-plot in the rear. On this latter my bedroom window looked; and never am I likely to forget the vile music of the cats throughout my first long

Dead Men Tell No Tales

wakeful night there. The second night they actually woke me; doubtless they had been busy long enough, but it was all of a sudden that I heard them, and lay listening for more, wide awake in an instant. My window had been very softly opened, and the draught fanned my forehead as I held my breath.

A faint light glimmered through a ground-glass pane over the door; and was dimly reflected by the toilet mirror, in its usual place against the window. This mirror I saw moved, and next moment I had bounded from bed.

The mirror fell with a horrid clatter: the toilet-table followed it with a worse: the thief had gone as he had come ere my toes halted aching amid the débris.

A useless little balcony—stone slab and iron railing—jutted out from my window. I thought I saw a hand on the railing, another on the slab, then both together on the lower level for one instant before they disappeared. There was a dull yet springy thud on the grass below. Then no more noise but the distant thunder of the traffic, and the one that woke me, until the window next mine was thrown up.

"What the devil's up?"

The voice was rich, cheery, light-hearted, agree-

I Find a Friend

able; all that my own was not as I answered "Nothing!" for this was not the first time my next-door neighbor had tried to scrape acquaintance with me.

"But surely, sir, I heard the very dickens of a row?"

"You may have done."

"I was afraid some one had broken into your room!"

"As a matter of fact," said I, put to shame by the undiminished good-humor of my neighbor, "some one did; but he's gone now, so let him be."

"Gone? Not he! He's getting over that wall. After him—after him!" And the head disappeared from the window next mine.

I rushed into the corridor, and was just in time to intercept a singularly handsome young fellow, at whom I had hardly taken the trouble to look until now. He was in full evening dress, and his face was radiant with the spirit of mischief and adventure.

"For God's sake, sir," I whispered, "let this matter rest. I shall have to come forward if you persist, and Heaven knows I have been before the public quite enough!"

His dark eyes questioned me an instant, then fell as though he would not disguise that he recollected

and understood. I liked him for his good taste.
I liked him for his tacit sympathy, and better still
for the amusing disappointment in his gallant,
young face.

"I am sorry to have robbed you of a pleasant
chase," said I. "At one time I should have been the
first to join you. But, to tell you the truth, I've had
enough excitement lately to last me for my life."

"I can believe that," he answered, with his fine
eyes full upon me. How strangely I had misjudged him! I saw no vulgar curiosity in his flattering gaze, but rather that very sympathy of which
I stood in need. I offered him my hand.

"It is very good of you to give in," I said. "No
one else has heard a thing, you see. I shall
look for another opportunity of thanking you to-
morrow."

"No, no!" cried he, "thanks be hanged, but—
but, I say, if I promise you not to bore you about
things—won't you drink a glass of brandy-and-
water in my room before you turn in again?"

Brandy-and-water being the very thing I needed,
and this young man pleasing me more and more,
I said that I would join him with all my heart,
and returned to my room for my dressing-gown
and slippers. To find them, however, I had to
light my candles, when the first thing I saw was

I Find a Friend

the havoc my marauder had left behind him. The mirror was cracked across; the dressing-table had lost a leg; and both lay flat, with my brushes and shaving-table, and the foolish toilet crockery which no one uses (but I should have to replace) strewn upon the carpet. But one thing I found that had not been there before: under the window lay a formidable sheath-knife without its sheath. I picked it up with something of a thrill, which did not lessen when I felt its edge. The thing was diabolically sharp. I took it with me to show my neighbor, whom I found giving his order to the boots; it seemed that it was barely midnight, and that he had only just come in when the clatter took place in my room.

"Hillo!" he cried, when the man was gone, and I produced my trophy. "Why, what the mischief have you got there?"

"My caller's card," said I. "He left it behind him. Feel the edge."

I have seldom seen a more indignant face than the one which my new acquaintance bent over the weapon, as he held it to the light, and ran his finger along the blade. He could have not frowned more heavily if he had recognized the knife.

"The villains!" he muttered. "The damned villains!"

"Villains?" I queried. "Did you see more than one of them, then?"

"Didn't you?" he asked quickly. "Yes, yes, to be sure! There was at least one other beggar skulking down below." He stood looking at me, the knife in his hand, though mine was held out for it. "Don't you think, Mr. Cole, that it's our duty to hand this over to the police? I—I've heard of other cases about these Inns of Court. There's evidently a gang of them, and this knife might convict the lot; there's no saying; anyway I think the police should have it. If you like I'll take it to Scotland Yard myself, and hand it over without mentioning your name."

"Oh, if you keep my name out of it," said I, "and say nothing about it here in the hotel, you may do what you like, and welcome! It's the proper course, no doubt; only I've had publicity, enough, and would sooner have felt that blade in my body than set my name going again in the newspapers."

"I understand," he said, with his well-bred sympathy, which never went a shade too far; and he dropped the weapon into a drawer, as the boots entered with the tray. In a minute he had brewed two steaming jorums of spirits-and-water; as he handed me one, I feared he was going to drink my

I Find a Friend

health, or toast my luck; but no, he was the one man I had met who seemed, as he said, to "understand." Nevertheless, he had his toast.

"Here's confusion to the criminal classes in general," he cried; "but death and damnation to the owners of that knife!"

And we clinked tumblers across the little oval table in the middle of the room. It was more of a sitting-room than mine; a bright fire was burning in the grate, and my companion insisted on my sitting over it in the arm-chair, while for himself he fetched the one from his bedside, and drew up the table so that our glasses should be handy. He then produced a handsome cigar-case admirably stocked, and we smoked and sipped in the cosiest fashion, though without exchanging many words.

You may imagine my pleasure in the society of a youth, equally charming in looks, manners and address, who had not one word to say to me about the *Lady Jermyn* or my hen-coop. It was unique Yet such, I suppose, was my native contrariety, that I felt I could have spoken of the catastrophe to this very boy with less reluctance than to any other creature whom I had encountered since my deliverance. He seemed so full of silent sympathy: his consideration for my feelings was so marked

73

Dead Men Tell No Tales

and yet so unobtrusive. I have called him a boy.
I am apt to write as the old man I have grown,
though I do believe I felt older then than now.
In any case my young friend was some years my
junior. I afterwards found out that he was six-
and-twenty.

I have also called him handsome. He was the
handsomest man that I have ever met, had the
frankest face, the finest eyes, the brightest smile.
Yet his bronzed forehead was low, and his mouth
rather impudent and bold than truly strong. And
there was a touch of foppery about him, in the
enormous white tie and the much-cherished whisk-
ers of the fifties, which was only redeemed by that
other touch of devilry that he had shown me in the
corridor. By the rich brown of his complexion,
as well as by a certain sort of swagger in his walk,
I should have said that he was a naval officer
ashore, had he not told me who he was of his own
accord.

"By the way," he said, "I ought to give you my
name. It's Rattray, of one of the many Kirby
Halls in this country. My one's down in Lancashire."

"I suppose there's no need to tell my name?"
said I, less sadly, I daresay, than I had ever yet
alluded to the tragedy which I alone survived. It

I Find a Friend

was an unnecessary allusion, too, as a reference to the foregoing conversation will show.

"Well, no," said he, in his frank fashion; "I can't honestly say there is."

We took a few puffs, he watching the fire, and I his firelit face.

"It must seem strange to you to be sitting with the only man who lived to tell the tale!"

The egotism of this speech was not wholly gratuitous. I thought it did seem strange to him: that a needless constraint was put upon him by excessive consideration for my feelings. I desired to set him at his ease as he had set me at mine. On the contrary, he seemed quite startled by my remark.

"It is strange," he said, with a shudder, followed by the biggest sip of brandy-and-water he had taken yet. "It must have been horrible—horrible!" he added to himself, his dark eyes staring into the fire.

"Ah!" said I, "it was even more horrible than you suppose or can ever imagine."

I was not thinking of myself, nor of my love, nor of any particular incident of the fire that still went on burning in my brain. My tone was doubtless confidential, but I was meditating no special confidence when my companion drew one with his next words. These, however, came after a pause, in which my eyes had fallen from his face, but in which I heard him emptying his glass.

"What do you mean?" he whispered. "That there were other circumstances—things which haven't got into the papers?"

"God knows there were," I answered, my face in my hands; and, my grief brought home to me, there I sat with it in the presence of that stranger, without compunction and without shame.

He sprang up and paced the room. His tact made me realize my weakness, and I was struggling to overcome it when he surprised me by suddenly stopping and laying a rather tremulous hand upon my shoulder.

"You—— It wouldn't do you any good to speak of those circumstances, I suppose?" he faltered.

"No: not now: no good at all."

"Forgive me," he said, resuming his walk. "I had no business—I felt so sorry—I cannot tell you how I sympathize! And yet—I wonder if you will always feel so?"

"No saying how I shall feel when I am a man again," said I. "You see what I am at present." And, pulling myself together, I rose to find my new friend quite agitated in his turn.

I Find a Friend

"I wish we had some more brandy," he sighed. "I'm afraid it's too late to get any now."

"And I'm glad of it," said I. "A man in my state ought not to look at spirits, or he may never look past them again. Thank goodness, there are other medicines. Only this morning I consulted the best man on nerves in London. I wish I'd gone to him long ago."

"Harley Street, was it?"

"Yes."

"Saw you on his doorstep, by Jove!" cried Rattray at once. "I was driving over to Hampstead, and I thought it was you. Well, what's the prescription?"

In my satisfaction at finding that he had not been dogging me intentionally (though I had forgotten the incident till he reminded me of it), I answered his question with unusual fulness.

"I should go abroad," said Rattray. "But then, I always am abroad; it's only the other day I got back from South America, and I shall up anchor again before this filthy English winter sets in."

Was he a sailor after all, or only a well-to-do wanderer on the face of the earth? He now mentioned that he was only in England for a few weeks, to have a look at his estate, and so forth; after which he plunged into more or less enthusiastic

Dead Men Tell No Tales

advocacy of this or that foreign resort, as opposed to the English cottage upon which I told him I had set my heart.

He was now, however, less spontaneous, I thought, than earlier in the night. His voice had lost its hearty ring, and he seemed preoccupied, as if talking of one matter while he thought upon another. Yet he would not let me go; and presently he confirmed my suspicion, no less than my first impression of his delightful frankness and cordiality, by candidly telling me what was on his mind.

"If you really want a cottage in the country," said he, "and the most absolute peace and quiet to be got in this world, I know of the very thing on my land in Lancashire. It would drive *me* mad in a week; but if you really care for that sort of thing——"

"An occupied cottage?" I interrupted.

"Yes; a couple rent it from me, very decent people of the name of Braithwaite. The man is out all day, and won't bother you when he's in; he's not like other people, poor chap. But the woman's all there, and would do her best for you in a humble, simple, wholesome sort of way."

"You think they would take me in?"

"They have taken other men—artists as a rule."

"Then it's a picturesque country?"

I Find a Friend

"Oh, it's that if it's nothing else; but not a town for miles, mind you, and hardly a village worthy the name."

"Any fishing?"

"Yes—trout—small but plenty of 'em—in a beck running close behind the cottage."

"Come," cried I, "this sounds delightful! Shall you be up there?"

"Only for a day or two," was the reply. "I shan't trouble you, Mr. Cole."

"My dear sir, that wasn't my meaning at all. I'm only sorry I shall not see something of you on your own heath. I can't thank you enough for your kind suggestion. When do you suppose the Braithwaites could do with me?"

His charming smile rebuked my impatience.

"We must first see whether they can do with you at all," said he. "I sincerely hope they can; but this is their time of year for tourists, though perhaps a little late. I'll tell you what I'll do. As a matter of fact, I'm going down there to-morrow, and I've got to telegraph to my place in any case to tell them when to meet me. I'll send the telegram first thing, and I'll make them send one back to say whether there's room in the cottage or not."

I thanked him warmly, but asked if the cottage

Dead Men Tell No Tales

was close to Kirby Hall, and whether this would
not be giving a deal of trouble at the other end;
whereupon he mischievously misunderstood me a
second time, saying the cottage and the hall were
not even in sight of each other, and I really had
no intrusion to fear, as he was a lonely bachelor
like myself, and would only be up there four or
five days at the most. So I made my appreciation
of his society plainer than ever to him; for indeed
I had found a more refreshing pleasure in it already than I had hoped to derive from mortal
man again; and we parted, at three o'clock in the
morning, like old fast friends.

"Only don't expect too much, my dear Mr.
Cole," were his last words to me. "My own place
is as ancient and as tumble-down as most ruins
that you pay to see over. And I'm never there
myself because—I tell you frankly—I hate it like
poison!"

CHAPTER VIII

A SMALL PRECAUTION

MY delight in the society of this young Squire Rattray (as I soon was to hear him styled) had been such as to make me almost forget the sinister incident which had brought us together. When I returned to my room, however, there were the open window and the litter on the floor to remind me of what had happened earlier in the night. Yet I was less disconcerted than you might suppose. A common housebreaker can have few terrors for one who has braved those of mid-ocean single-handed; my would-be visitor had no longer any for me; for it had not yet occurred to me to connect him with the voices and the footsteps to which, indeed, I had been unable to swear before the doctor. On the other hand, these morbid imaginings (as I was far from unwilling to consider them) had one and all deserted me in the sane, clean company of the capital young fellow in the next room.

I have confessed my condition up to the time of this queer meeting. I have tried to bring young

Dead Men Tell No Tales

Rattray before you with some hint of his fresh-
ness and his boyish charm; and though the sense
of failure is heavy upon me there, I who knew the
man knew also that I must fail to do him justice.
Enough may have been said, however, to impart
some faint idea of what this youth was to me in
the bitter and embittering anti-climax of my life.
Conventional figures spring to my pen, but every
one of them is true; he was flowers in spring, he
was sunshine after rain, he was rain following
long months of drought. I slept admirably after
all; and I awoke to see the overturned toilet-table,
and to thrill as I remembered there was one
fellow-creature with whom I could fraternize without fear of a rude reopening of my every wound.

I hurried my dressing in the hope of our break-
fasting together. I knocked at the next door, and,
receiving no answer, even ventured to enter, with
the same idea. He was not there. He was not
in the coffee-room. He was not in the hotel.

I broke my fast in disappointed solitude, and
I hung about disconsolate all the morning, looking wistfully for my new-made friend. Towards
mid-day he drove up in a cab which he kept waiting at the curb.

"It's all right!" he cried out in his hearty way.
"I sent my telegram first thing, and I've had the

A Small Precaution

answer at my club. The rooms are vacant, and I'll see that Jane Braithwaite has all ready for you by to-morrow night."

I thanked him from my heart. "You seem in a hurry!" I added, as I followed him up the stairs.

"I am," said he. "It's a near thing for the train. I've just time to stick in my things."

"Then I'll stick in mine," said I impulsively, "and I'll come with you, and doss down in any corner for the night."

He stopped and turned on the stairs.

"You mustn't do that," said he; "they won't have anything ready. I'm going to make it my privilege to see that everything is. as cosey as possible when you arrive. I simply can't allow you to come to-day, Mr. Cole!" He smiled, but I saw that he was in earnest, and of course I gave in.

"All right," said I; "then I must content myself with seeing you off at the station."

To my surprise his smile faded, and a flush of undisguised annoyance made him, if anything, better-looking than ever. It brought out a certain strength of mouth and jaw which I had not observed there hitherto. It gave him an ugliness of expression which only emphasized his perfection of feature.

"You mustn't do that either," said he, shortly.

Dead Men Tell No Tales

"I have an appointment at the station. I shall be talking business all the time."

He was gone to his room, and I went to mine feeling duly snubbed; yet I deserved it; for I had exhibited a characteristic (though not chronic) want of taste, of which I am sometimes guilty to this day. Not to show ill-feeling on the head of it, I nevertheless followed him down again in four or five minutes. And I was rewarded by his brightest smile as he grasped my hand.

"Come to-morrow by the same train," said he, naming station, line, and hour; "unless I telegraph, all will be ready and you shall be met. You may rely on reasonable charges. As to the fishing, go up-stream—to the right when you strike the beck—and you'll find a good pool or two. I may have to go to Lancaster the day after to-morrow, but I shall give you a call when I get back."

With that we parted, as good friends as ever. I observed that my regret at losing him was shared by the boots, who stood beside me on the steps as his hansom rattled off.

"I suppose Mr. Rattray stays here always when he comes to town?" said I.

"No, sir," said the man, "we've never had him before, not in my time; but I shouldn't mind if he came again." And he looked twice at the coin in his hand before pocketing it with evident satisfaction.

Lonely as I was, and wished to be, I think that I never felt my loneliness as I did during the twenty-four hours which intervened between Rattray's departure and my own. They dragged like wet days by the sea, and the effect was as depressing. I have seldom been at such a loss for something to do; and in my idleness I behaved like a child, wishing my new friend back again, or myself on the railway with my new friend, until I blushed for the beanstalk growth of my regard for him, an utter stranger, and a younger man. I am less ashamed of it now: he had come into my dark life like a lamp, and his going left a darkness deeper than before.

In my dejection I took a new view of the night's outrage. It was no common burglar's work, for what had I worth stealing? It was the work of my unseen enemies, who dogged me in the street; they alone knew why; the doctor had called these hallucinations, and I had forced myself to agree with the doctor; but I could not deceive myself in my present mood. I remembered the steps, the steps—the stopping when I stopped—the drawing away in the crowded streets—the closing up in

quieter places. Why had I never looked round?
Why? Because till to-day I had thought it mere
vulgar curiosity; because a few had bored me, I
had imagined the many at my heels; but now I
knew—I knew! It was the few again: a few who
hated me even unto death.

The idea took such a hold upon me that I did
not trouble my head with reasons and motives.
Certain persons had designs upon my life; that
was enough for me. On the whole, the thought
was stimulating; it set a new value on existence,
and it roused a certain amount of spirit even in
me. I would give the fellows another chance
before I left town. They should follow me once
more, and this time to some purpose. Last night
they had left a knife on me; to-night I would
have a keepsake ready for them.

Hitherto I had gone unarmed since my landing, which, perhaps, was no more than my duty
as a civilized citizen. On Black Hill Flats, however, I had formed another habit, of which I
should never have broken myself so easily, but
for the fact that all the firearms I ever had were
reddening and rotting at the bottom of the Atlantic Ocean. I now went out and bought me such
a one as I had never possessed before.

The revolver was then in its infancy; but it

A Small Precaution

did exist; and by dusk I was owner of as fine a specimen as could be procured in the city of London. It had but five chambers, but the barrel was ten inches long; one had to cap it, and to put in the powder and the wadded bullet separately; but the last-named would have killed an elephant. The oak case that I bought with it cumbers my desk as I write, and, shut, you would think that it had never contained anything more lethal than fruit-knives. I open it, and there are the green-baize compartments, one with a box of percussion caps, still apparently full, another that could not contain many more wadded-bullets, and a third with a powder-horn which can never have been much lighter. Within the lid is a label bearing the makers' names; the gentlemen themselves are unknown to me, even if they are still alive; nevertheless, after five-and-forty years, let me dip my pen to Messrs. Deane, Adams and Deane!

That night I left this case in my room, locked, and the key in my waistcoat pocket; in the right-hand side-pocket of my overcoat I carried my Deane and Adams, loaded in every chamber; also my right hand, as innocently as you could wish. And just that night I was not followed! I walked across Regent's Park, and I dawdled on Primrose Hill, without the least result. Down I turned into

the Avenue Road, and presently was strolling between green fields towards Finchley. The moon
was up, but nicely shaded by a thin coating of
clouds which extended across the sky: it was an
ideal night for it. It was also my last night in
town, and I did want to give the beggars their
last chance. But they did not even attempt to
avail themselves of it: never once did they follow
me: my ears were in too good training to make
any mistake. And the reason only dawned on me
as I drove back disappointed: they had followed
me already to the gunsmith's!

Convinced of this, I entertained but little hope
of another midnight visitor. Nevertheless, I put
my light out early, and sat a long time peeping
through my blind; but only an inevitable Tom,
with back hunched up and tail erect, broke the
moonlit profile of the back-garden wall; and once
more that disreputable music (which none the less
had saved my life) was the only near sound all
night.

I felt very reluctant to pack Deane and Adams
away in his case next morning, and the case in
my portmanteau, where I could not get at it in
case my unknown friends took it into their heads
to accompany me out of town. In the hope that
they would, I kept him loaded, and in the same

A Small Precaution

overcoat pocket, until late in the afternoon, when, being very near my northern destination, and having the compartment to myself, I locked the toy away with considerable remorse for the price I had paid for it. All down the line I had kept an eye for suspicious characters with an eye upon me; but even my self-consciousness failed to discover one; and I reached my haven of peace, and of fresh fell air, feeling, I suppose, much like any other fool who has spent his money upon a white elephant.

CHAPTER IX

MY CONVALESCENT HOME

THE man Braithwaite met me at the station with a spring cart. The very porters seemed to expect me, and my luggage was in the cart before I had given up my ticket. Nor had we started when I first noticed that Braithwaite did not speak when I spoke to him. On the way, however, a more flagrant instance recalled young Rattray's remark, that the man was "not like other people." I had imagined it to refer to a mental, not a physical, defect; whereas it was clear to me now that my prospective landlord was stone-deaf, and I presently discovered him to be dumb as well. Thereafter I studied him with some attention during our drive of four or five miles. I called to mind the theory that an innate physical deficiency is seldom without its moral counterpart, and I wondered how far this would apply to the deaf-mute at my side, who was ill-grown, wizened, and puny into the bargain. The brow-beaten face of him was certainly forbidding, and he thrashed his horse up the hills in a dogged, vindictive,

My Convalescent Home

thorough-going way which at length made me jump out and climb one of them on foot. It was the only form of protest that occurred to me.

The evening was damp and thick. It melted into night as we drove. I could form no impression of the country, but this seemed desolate enough. I believe we met no living soul on the high road which we followed for the first three miles or more. At length we turned into a narrow lane, with a stiff stone wall on either hand, and this eventually led us past the lights of what appeared to be a large farm; it was really a small hamlet; and now we were nearing our destination. Gates had to be opened, and my poor driver breathed hard from the continual getting down and up. In the end a long and heavy cart-track brought us to the loneliest light that I have ever seen. It shone on the side of a hill—in the heart of an open wilderness—as solitary as a beacon-light at sea. It was the light of the cottage which was to be my temporary home.

A very tall, gaunt woman stood in the doorway against the inner glow. She advanced with a loose, long stride, and invited me to enter in a voice harsh (I took it) from disuse. I was warming myself before the kitchen fire when she came in carrying my heaviest box as though it had nothing in it. I ran to take it from her, for the box was full of books, but she shook her head, and was on the stairs with it before I could intercept her.

I conceive that very few men are attracted by abnormal strength in a woman; we cannot help it; and yet it was not her strength which first repelled me in Mrs. Braithwaite. It was a combination of attributes. She had a poll of very dirty and untidy red hair; her eyes were set close together; she had the jowl of the traditional prizefighter. But far more disagreeable than any single feature was the woman's expression, or rather the expression which I caught her assuming naturally, and banishing with an effort for my benefit. To me she was strenuously civil in her uncouth way. But I saw her give her husband one look, as he staggered in with my comparatively light portmanteau, which she instantly snatched out of his feeble arms. I saw this look again before the evening was out, and it was such a one as Braithwaite himself had fixed upon his horse as he flogged it up the hills.

I began to wonder how the young squire had found it in his conscience to recommend such a pair. I wondered less when the woman finally ushered me upstairs to my rooms. These were

My Convalescent Home

small and rugged, but eminently snug and clean.
In each a good fire blazed cheerfully; my portmanteau was already unstrapped, the table in the
sitting-room already laid; and I could not help
looking twice at the silver and the glass, so bright
was their condition, so good their quality. Mrs.
Braithwaite watched me from the door.

"I doubt you'll be thinking them's our own,"
said she. "I wish they were; t'squire sent 'em in
this afternoon."

"For my use?"

"Ay; I doubt he thought what we had ourselves
wasn't good enough. An' it's him 'at sent t'arm-
chair, t'bed-linen, t'bath, an' that there lookin'-
glass an' all."

She had followed me into the bedroom, where
I looked with redoubled interest at each object
as she mentioned it, and it was in the glass—a
masqueline shaving-glass—that I caught my second glimpse of my landlady's evil expression—
levelled this time at myself.

I instantly turned round and told her that I
thought it very kind of Mr. Rattray, but that, for
my part, I was not a luxurious man, and that I
felt rather sorry the matter had not been left entirely in her hands. She retired seemingly mol-
lified, and she took my sympathy with her, though

Dead Men Tell No Tales

I was none the less pleased and cheered by my new friend's zeal for my comfort; there were even flowers on my table, without a doubt from Kirby Hall.

And in another matter the squire had not misled me: the woman was an excellent plain cook. I expected ham and eggs. Sure enough, this was my dish, but done to a turn. The eggs were new and all unbroken, the ham so lean and yet so tender, that I would not have exchanged my humble, hearty meal for the best dinner served that night in London. It made a new man of me, after my long journey and my cold, damp drive. I was for chatting with Mrs. Braithwaite when she came up to clear away. I thought she might be glad to talk after the life she must lead with her afflicted husband, but it seemed to have had the opposite effect on her. All I elicited was an ambiguous statement as to the distance between the cottage and the hall; it was "not so far." And so she left me to my pipe and to my best night yet, in the stillest spot I have ever slept in on dry land; one heard nothing but the bubble of a beck; and it seemed very, very far away.

A fine, bright morning showed me my new surroundings in their true colors; even in the sunshine these were not very gay. But gayety was

My Convalescent Home

the last thing I wanted. Peace and quiet were my whole desire, and both were here, set in scenery at once lovely to the eye and bracing to the soul.

From the cottage doorstep one looked upon a perfect panorama of healthy, open English country. Purple hills hemmed in a broad, green, undulating plateau, scored across and across by the stone walls of the north, and all dappled with the shadows of rolling leaden clouds with silver fringes. Miles away a church spire stuck like a spike out of the hollow, and the smoke of a village dimmed the trees behind. No nearer habitation could I see. I have mentioned a hamlet which we passed in the spring-cart. It lay hidden behind some hillocks to the left. My landlady told me it was better than half a mile away, and "nothing when you get there; no shop; no post-office; not even a public-house."

I inquired in which direction lay the hall. She pointed to the nearest trees, a small forest of stunted oaks, which shut in the view to the right, after quarter of a mile of a bare and rugged valley. Through this valley twisted the beck which I had heard faintly in the night. It ran through the oak plantation and so to the sea, some two or three miles further on, said my landlady; but nobody would have thought it was so near.

Dead Men Tell No Tales

"T'squire was to be away to-day," observed the woman, with the broad vowel sound which I shall not attempt to reproduce in print. "He was going to Lancaster, I believe."

"So I understood," said I. "I didn't think of troubling him, if that's what you mean. I'm going to take his advice and fish the beck."

And I proceeded to do so after a hearty early dinner: the keen, chill air was doing me good already: the "perfect quiet" was finding its way into my soul. I blessed my specialist, I blessed Squire Rattray, I blessed the very villains who had brought us within each other's ken; and nowhere was my thanksgiving more fervent than in the deep cleft threaded by the beck; for here the shrewd yet gentle wind passed completely overhead, and the silence was purged of oppression by the ceaseless symphony of clear water running over clean stones.

But it was no day for fishing, and no place for the fly, though I went through the form of throwing one for several hours. Here the stream merely rinsed its bed, there it stood so still, in pools of liquid amber, that, when the sun shone, the very pebbles showed their shadows in the deepest places. Of course I caught nothing; but, towards

My Convalescent Home

the close of the gold-brown afternoon, I made yet
another new acquaintance, in the person of a little
old clergyman who attacked me pleasantly from
the rear.

"Bad day for fishing, sir," croaked the cheery
voice which first informed me of his presence.
"Ah, I knew it must be a stranger," he cried as
I turned and he hopped down to my side with the
activity of a much younger man.

"Yes," I said, "I only came down from London
yesterday. I find the spot so delightful that I
haven't bothered much about the sport. Still, I've
had about enough of it now." And I prepared to
take my rod to pieces.

"Spot and sport!" laughed the old gentleman.
"Didn't mean it for a pun, I hope? Never could
endure puns! So you came down yesterday, young
gentleman, did you? And where may you be
staying?"

I described the position of my cottage without
the slightest hesitation; for this parson did not
scare me; except in appearance he had so little in
common with his type as I knew it. He had,
however, about the shrewdest pair of eyes that I
have ever seen, and my answer only served to
intensify their open scrutiny.

"How on earth did you come to hear of a God-forsaken place like this?" said he, making use, I thought, of a somewhat stronger expression than quite became his cloth.

"Squire Rattray told me of it," said I.

"Ha! So you're a friend of his, are you?" And his eyes went through and through me, like knitting-needles through a ball of wool.

"I could hardly call myself that," said I. "But Mr. Rattray has been very kind to me."

"Meet him in town?"

I said I had, but I said it with some coolness, for his tone had dropped into the confidential, and I disliked it as much as this string of questions from a stranger.

"Long ago, sir?" he pursued.

"No, sir; not long ago," I retorted.

"May I ask your name?" said he.

"You may ask what you like," I cried, with a final reversal of all my first impressions of this impertinent old fellow; "but I'm hanged if I tell it you! I am here for rest and quiet, sir. I don't ask you your name. I can't for the life of me see what right you have to ask me mine, or to question me at all, for that matter."

He favored me with a brief glance of extraordinary suspicion. It faded away in mere surprise, and, next instant, my elderly and reverend friend

My Convalescent Home

was causing me some compunction by coloring like a boy.

"You may think my curiosity mere impertinence, sir," said he; "you would think otherwise if you knew as much as I do of Squire Rattray's friends, and how little you resemble the generality of them. You might even feel some sympathy for one of the neighboring clergy, to whom this godless young man has been for years as a thorn in their side."

He spoke so gravely, and what he said was so easy to believe, that I could not but apologize for my hasty words.

"Don't name it, sir," said the clergyman; "you had a perfect right to resent my questions, and I enjoy meeting young men of spirit; but not when it's an evil spirit, such as, I fear, possesses your friend! I do assure you, sir, that the best thing I have heard of him for years is the very little that you have told me. As a rule, to hear of him at all in this part of the world, is to wish that we had not heard. I see him coming, however, and shall detain you no longer, for I don't deny that there is no love lost between us."

I looked round, and there was Rattray on the top of the bank, a long way to the left, coming towards me with a waving hat. An extraor-

Dead Men Tell No Tales

dinary ejaculation brought me to the right-about next instant.

The old clergyman had slipped on a stone in mid-stream, and, as he dragged a dripping leg up the opposite bank, he had sworn an oath worthy of the "godless young man" who had put him to flight, and on whose demerits he had descanted with so much eloquence and indignation.

CHAPTER X

WINE AND WEAKNESS

"SPORTING old parson who knows how to swear?" laughed Rattray. "Never saw him in my life before; wondered who the deuce he was."

"Really?" said I. "He professed to know something of you."

"Against me, you mean? My dear Cole, don't trouble to perjure yourself. I don't mind, believe me. They're easily shocked, these country clergy, and no doubt I'm a bugbear to 'em. Yet, I could have sworn I'd never seen this one before. Let's have another look."

We were walking away together. We turned on the top of the bank. And there the old clergyman was planted on the moorside, and watching us intently from under his hollowed hands.

"Well, I'm hanged!" exclaimed Rattray, as the hands fell and their owner beat a hasty retreat. My companion said no more; indeed, for some minutes we pursued our way in silence. And I thought that it was with an effort that he broke

Dead Men Tell No Tales

into sudden inquiries concerning my journey and my comfort at the cottage.

This gave me an opportunity of thanking him for his little attentions. "It was awfully good of you," said I, taking his arm as though I had known him all my life; nor do I think there was another living man with whom I would have linked arms at that time.

"Good?" cried he. "Nonsense, my dear sir! I'm only afraid you find it devilish rough. But, at all events, you're coming to dine with me to-night."

"Am I?" I asked, smiling.

"Rather!" said he. "My time here is short enough. I don't lose sight of you again between this and midnight."

"It's most awfully good of you," said I again.

"Wait till you see! You'll find it rough enough at my place; all my retainers are out for the day at a local show."

"Then I certainly shall not give you the trouble——"

He interrupted me with his jovial laugh.

"My good fellow," he cried, "that's the fun of it! How do you suppose I've been spending the day? Told you I was going to Lancaster, did I? Well, I've been cooking our dinner in-

102

Wine and Weakness

stead—laying the table—getting up the wines—
never had such a joke! Give you my word, I
almost forgot I was in the wilderness!"

"So you're quite alone, are you?"

"Yes; as much so as that other beggar who
was monarch of all he surveyed, his right there
was none to dispute, from the what-is-it down to
the glade——"

"I'll come," said I, as we reached the cottage.
"Only first you must let me make myself decent."

"You're decent enough!"

"My boots are wet; my hands——"

"All serene! I'll give you five minutes."

And I left him outside, flourishing a handsome
watch, while, on my way upstairs, I paused to tell
Mrs. Braithwaite that I was dining at the hall.
She was busy cooking, and I felt prepared for
her unpleasant expression; but she showed no
annoyance at my news. I formed the impression
that it was no news to her. And next minute I
heard a whispering below; it was unmistakable in
that silent cottage, where not a word had reached
me yet, save in conversation to which I was myself a party.

I looked out of window. Rattray I could no
longer see. And I confess that I felt both puz-
zled and annoyed until we walked away together,

when it was his arm which was immediately thrust through mine.

"A good soul, Jane," said he; "though she made an idiotic marriage, and leads a life which might spoil the temper of an archangel. She was my nurse when I was a youngster, Cole, and we never meet without a yarn." Which seemed natural enough; still I failed to perceive why they need yarn in whispers.

Kirby Hall proved startlingly near at hand. We descended the bare valley to the right, we crossed the beck upon a plank, were in the oak-plantation about a minute, and there was the hall upon the farther side.

And a queer old place it seemed, half farm, half feudal castle: fowls strutting at large about the back premises (which we were compelled to skirt), and then a front door of ponderous oak, deep-set between walls fully six feet thick, and studded all over with wooden pegs. The façade, indeed, was wholly grim, with a castellated tower at one end, and a number of narrow, sunken windows looking askance on the wreck and ruin of a once prim, old-fashioned, high-walled garden. I thought that Rattray might have shown more respect for the house of his ancestors. It put me in mind of a neglected grave. And yet I could forgive a bright young fellow for never coming near so desolate a domain.

We dined delightfully in a large and lofty hall, formerly used (said Rattray) as a court-room. The old judgment seat stood back against the wall, and our table was the one at which the justices had been wont to sit. Then the chamber had been low-ceiled; now it ran to the roof, and we ate our dinner beneath a square of fading autumn sky, with I wondered how many ghosts looking down on us from the oaken gallery! I was interested, impressed, awed not a little, and yet all in a way which afforded my mind the most welcome distraction from itself and from the past. To Rattray, on the other hand, it was rather sadly plain that the place was both a burden and a bore; in fact he vowed it was the dampest and the dullest old ruin under the sun, and that he would sell it to-morrow if he could find a lunatic to buy. His want of sentiment struck me as his one deplorable trait. Yet even this displayed his characteristic merit of frankness. Nor was it at all unpleasant to hear his merry, boyish laughter ringing round hall and gallery, ere it died away against a dozen closed doors.

And there were other elements of good cheer: a log fire blazing heartily in the old dog-grate, casting a glow over the stone flags, a reassuring flicker into the darkest corner: cold viands of the very best: and the finest old Madeira that has ever passed my lips.

"Now, all my life I have been a "moderate drinker" in the most literal sense of that slightly elastic term. But at the sad time of which I am trying to write, I was almost an abstainer, from the fear, the temptation—of seeking oblivion in strong waters. To give way then was to go on giving way. I realized the danger, and I took stern measures. Not stern enough, however; for what I did not realize was my weak and nervous state, in which a glass would have the same effect on me as three or four upon a healthy man.

Heaven knows how much or how little I took that evening! I can swear it was the smaller half of either bottle—and the second we never finished—but the amount matters nothing. Even me it did not make grossly tipsy. But it warmed my blood, it cheered my heart, it excited my brain, and— it loosened my tongue. It set me talking with a freedom of which I should have been incapable in my normal moments, on a subject whereof I had never before spoken of my own free will.

And yet the will to speak—to my present companion—was no novelty. I had felt it at our first meeting in the private hotel. His tact, his sympathy, his handsome face, his personal charm, his frank friendliness, had one and all tempted me to bore this complete stranger with unsolicited confidences for which an inquisitive relative might have angled in vain. And the temptation was the stronger because I knew in my heart that I should not bore the young squire at all; that he was anxious enough to hear my story from my own lips, but too good a gentleman intentionally to betray such anxiety. Vanity was also in the impulse. A vulgar newspaper prominence had been my final (and very genuine)tribulation; but to please and to interest one so pleasing and so interesting to me, was another and a subtler thing. And then there was his sympathy—shall I add his admiration?—for my reward.

I do not pretend that I argued thus deliberately in my heated and excited brain. I merely hold that all these small reasons and motives were there, fused and exaggerated by the liquor which was there as well. Nor can I say positively that Rattray put no leading questions; only that I remember none which had that sound; and that, once started, I am afraid I needed only too little encouragement to run on and on.

Dead Men Tell No Tales

Well, I was set going before we got up from the table. I continued in an armchair that my host dragged from a little book-lined room adjoining the hall. I finished on my legs, my back to the fire, my hands beating wildly together. I had told my dear Rattray of my own accord more than living man had extracted from me yet. He interrupted me very little; never once until I came to the murderous attack by Santos on the drunken steward.

"The brute!" cried Rattray. "The cowardly, cruel, foreign devil! And you never let out one word of that!"

"What was the good?" said I. "They are all gone now—all gone to their account. Every man of us was a brute at the last. There was nothing to be gained by telling the public that."

He let me go on until I came to another point which I had hitherto kept to myself: the condition of the dead mate's fingers: the cries that the sight of them had recalled.

"That Portuguese villain again!" cried my companion, fairly leaping from the chair which I had left and he had taken. "It was the work of the same cane that killed the steward. Don't tell me an Englishman would have done it; and yet you said nothing about that either!"

Wine and Weakness

It was my first glimpse of this side of my young host's character. Nor did I admire him the less, in his spirited indignation, because much of this was clearly against myself. His eyes flashed. His face was white. I suddenly found myself the cooler man of the two.

"My dear fellow, do consider!" said I. "What possible end could have been served by my stating what I couldn't prove against a man who could never be brought to book in this world? Santos was punished as he deserved; his punishment was death, and there's an end on't."

"You might be right," said Rattray, "but it makes my blood boil to hear such a story. Forgive me if I have spoken strongly;" and he paced his hall for a little in an agitation which made me like him better and better. "The cold-blooded villain!" he kept muttering; "the infernal, foreign, blood-thirsty rascal! Perhaps you were right; it couldn't have done any good, I know; but—I only wish he'd lived for us to hang him, Cole! Why, a beast like that is capable of anything: I wonder if you've told me the worst even now?" And he stood before me, with candid suspicion in his fine, frank eyes.

"What makes you say that?" said I, rather nettled.

Dead Men Tell No Tales

"I shan't tell you if it's going to rile you, old fellow," was his reply. And with it reappeared the charming youth whom I found it impossible to resist. "Heaven knows you have had enough to worry you!" he added, in his kindly, sympathetic voice.

"So much," said I, "that you cannot add to it, my dear Rattray. Now, then! Why do you think there was something worse?"

"You hinted as much in town: rightly or wrongly I gathered there was something you would never speak about to living man."

I turned from him with a groan.

"Ah! but that had nothing to do with Santos."

"Are you sure?" he cried.

"No," I murmured; "it *had* something to do with him, in a sense; but don't ask me any more." And I leaned my forehead on the high oak mantelpiece, and groaned again.

His hand was upon my shoulder.

"Do tell me," he urged. I was silent. He pressed me further. In my fancy, both hand and voice shook with his sympathy.

"He had a step-daughter," said I at last.

"Yes? Yes?"

"I loved her. That was all."

Wine and Weakness

His hand dropped from my shoulder. I remained standing, stooping, thinking only of her whom I had lost for ever. The silence was intense. I could hear the wind sighing in the oaks without, the logs burning softly away at my feet. And so we stood until the voice of Rattray recalled me from the deck of the *Lady Jermyn* and my lost love's side.

"So that was all!"

I turned and met a face I could not read.

"Was it not enough?" cried I. "What more would you have?"

"I expected some more—foul play!"

"Ah!" I exclaimed bitterly. "So that was all that interested you! No, there was no more foul play that I know of; and if there was, I don't care. Nothing matters to me but one thing. Now that you know what that is, I hope you're satisfied."

It was no way to speak to one's host. Yet I felt that he had pressed me unduly. I hated myself for my final confidence, and his want of sympathy made me hate him too. In my weakness, however, I was the natural prey of violent extremes. His hand flew out to me. He was about to speak. A moment more and I had doubtless forgiven him. But another sound came instead and made the pair of us start and stare. It was the soft shutting of some upstairs door.

"I thought we had the house to ourselves?" cried I, my miserable nerves on edge in an instant.

"So did I," he answered, very pale. "My servants must have come back. By the Lord Harry, they shall hear of this!"

He sprang to a door, I heard his feet clattering up some stone stairs, and in a trice he was running along the gallery overhead; in another I heard him railing behind some upper door that he had flung open and banged behind him; then his voice dropped, and finally died away. I was left some minutes in the oppressively silent hall, shaken, startled, ashamed of my garrulity, aching to get away. When he returned it was by another of the many closed doors, and he found me awaiting him, hat in hand. He was wearing his happiest look until he saw my hat.

"Not going?" he cried. "My dear Cole, I can't apologize sufficiently for my abrupt desertion of you, much less for the cause. It was my man, just come in from the show, and gone up the back way. I accused him of listening to our conversation. Of course he denies it; but it really doesn't matter, as I'm sorry to say he's much too 'fresh' (as they call it down here) to remember

Wine and Weakness

anything to-morrow morning. I let him have it, I can tell you. Varlet! Caitiff! But if you bolt off on the head of it, I shall go back and sack him into the bargain!"

I assured him I had my own reasons for wishing to retire early. He could have no conception of my weakness, my low and nervous condition of body and mind; much as I had enjoyed myself, he must really let me go. Another glass of wine, then? Just one more? No, I had drunk too much already. I was in no state to stand it. And I held out my hand with decision.

Instead of taking it he looked at me very hard.

"The place doesn't suit you," said he. "I see it doesn't, and I'm devilish sorry! Take my advice and try something milder; now do, to-morrow; for I should never forgive myself if it made you worse instead of better; and the air *is* too strong for lots of people."

I was neither too ill nor too vexed to laugh outright in his face.

"It's not the air," said I; "it's that splendid old Madeira of yours, *that* was too strong for me, if you like! No, no, Rattray, you don't get rid of me so cheaply—much as you seem to want to!"

"I was only thinking of you," he rejoined, with a touch of pique that convinced me of his sincerity.

Dead Men Tell No Tales

"Of course I want you to stop, though I shan't be here many days; but I feel responsible for you, Cole, and that's the fact. Think you can find your way?" he continued, accompanying me to the gate, a postern in the high garden wall. "Hadn't you better have a lantern?"

No; it was unnecessary. I could see splendidly, had the bump of locality and as many more lies as would come to my tongue. I was indeed burning to be gone.

A moment later I feared that I had shown this too plainly. For his final handshake was hearty enough to send me away something ashamed of my precipitancy, and with a further sense of having shown him small gratitude for his kindly anxiety on my behalf. I would behave differently tomorrow. Meanwhile I had new regrets.

At first it was comparatively easy to see, for the lights of the house shone faintly among the nearer oaks. But the moon was hidden behind heavy clouds, and I soon found myself at a loss in a terribly dark zone of timber. Already I had left the path. I felt in my pocket for matches. I had none.

My head was now clear enough, only deservedly heavy. I was still quarrelling with myself for my indiscretions and my incivilities, one and all the

Wine and Weakness

result of his wine and my weakness, and this new predicament (another and yet more vulgar result) was the final mortification. I swore aloud. I simply could not see a foot in front of my face. Once I proved it by running my head hard against a branch. I was hopelessly and ridiculously lost within a hundred yards of the hall!

Some minutes I floundered, ashamed to go back, unable to proceed for the trees and the darkness. I heard the beck running over its stones. I could still see an occasional glimmer from the windows I had left. But the light was now on this side, now on that; the running water chuckled in one ear after the other; there was nothing for it but to return in all humility for the lantern which I had been so foolish as to refuse.

And as I resigned myself to this imperative though inglorious course, my heart warmed once more to the jovial young squire. He would laugh, but not unkindly, at my grotesque dilemma; at the thought of his laughter I began to smile myself. If he gave me another chance I would smoke that cigar with him before starting home afresh, and remove, from my own mind no less than from his, all ill impressions. After all it was not his fault that I had taken too much of his wine; but a far worse offence was to be sulky

Dead Mell Tell No Tales

in one's cups. I would show him that I was myself again in all respects. I have admitted that
I was temporarily, at all events, a creature of extreme moods. It was in this one that I retraced
my steps towards the lights, and at length let
myself into the garden by the postern at which I
had shaken Rattray's hand not ten minutes before.

Taking heart of grace, I stepped up jauntily to
the porch. The weeds muffled my steps. I myself had never thought of doing so, when all at
once I halted in a vague terror. Through the
deep lattice windows I had seen into the lighted
hall. And Rattray was once more seated at his
table, a little company of men around him.

I crept nearer, and my heart stopped. Was I
delirious, or raving mad with wine? Or had the
sea given up its dead?

CHAPTER XI

I LIVE AGAIN

SQUIRE RATTRAY, as I say, was seated at the head of his table, where the broken meats still lay as he and I had left them; his fingers, I remember, were playing with a crust, and his eyes fixed upon a distant door, as he leant back in his chair. Behind him hovered the nigger of the *Lady Jermyn,* whom I had been the slower to recognize, had not her skipper sat facing me on the squire's right. Yes, there was Captain Harris in the flesh, eating heartily between great gulps of wine, instead of feeding the fishes as all the world supposed. And nearer still, nearer me than any, with his back to my window but his chair slued round a little, so that he also could see that door, and I his profile, sat Joaquin Santos with his cigarette!

None spoke; all seemed waiting; and all were silent but the captain, whose vulgar champing reached me through the crazy lattice, as I stood spellbound and petrified without.

They say that a drowning man lives his life

Dead Men Tell No Tales

again before the last; but my own fight with the
sea provided me with no such moments of vivid
and rapid retrospect as those during which I stood
breathless outside the lighted windows of Kirby
Hall. I landed again. I was dogged day and
night. I set it down to nerves and notoriety; but
took refuge in a private hotel. One followed me,
engaged the next room, set a watch on all my
movements; another came in by the window to
murder me in my bed; no party to that, the first
one nevertheless turned the outrage to account,
wormed himself into my friendship on the strength
of it, and lured me hither, an easy prey. And here
was the gang of them, to meet me! No wonder
Rattray had not let me see him off at the station;
no wonder I had not been followed that night.
Every link I saw in its right light instantly. Only
the motive remained obscure. Suspicious circumstances swarmed upon my slow perception: how
innocent I had been! Less innocent, however,
than wilfully and wholly reckless: what had it
mattered with whom I made friends? What had
anything mattered to me? What did anything
matter—

I thought my heart had snapped!

Why were they watching that door, Joaquin
Santos and the young squire? Whom did they

I Live Again

await? I knew! Oh, I knew! My heart leaped, my blood danced, my eyes lay in wait with theirs. Everything began to matter once more. It was as though the machinery of my soul, long stopped, had suddenly been set in motion; it was as though I was born again.

How long we seemed to wait I need not say. It cannot have been many moments in reality, for Santos was blowing his rings of smoke in the direction of the door, and the first that I noticed were but dissolving when it opened—and the best was true! One instant I saw her very clearly, in the light of a candle which she carried in its silver stick; then a mist blinded me, and I fell on my knees in the rank bed into which I had stepped, to give such thanks to the Almighty as this heart has never felt before or since. And I remained kneeling; for now my face was on a level with the sill; and when my eyes could see again, there stood my darling before them in the room.

Like a queen she stood, in the very travelling cloak in which I had seen her last; it was tattered now, but she held it close about her as though a shrewd wind bit her to the core. Her sweet face was all peeked and pale in the candle-light: she who had been a child was come to womanhood in a few weeks. But a new spirit flashed in her

Dead Men Tell No Tales

dear eyes, a new strength hardened her young lips. She stood as an angel brought to book by devils; and so noble was her calm defiance, so serene her scorn, that, as I watched and listened, all present fear for her passed out of my heart.

The first sound was the hasty rising of young Rattray; he was at Eva's side next instant, essaying to lead her to his chair, with a flush which deepened as she repulsed him coldly.

"You have sent for me, and I have come," said she. "But I prefer not to sit down in your presence; and what you have to say, you will be good enough to say as quickly as possible, that I may go again before I am—stifled!"

It was her one hot word; aimed at them all, it seemed to me to fall like a lash on Rattray's cheek, bringing the blood to it like lightning. But it was Santos who snatched the cigarette from his mouth, and opened upon the defenceless girl in a torrent of Portuguese, yellow with rage, and a very windmill of lean arms and brown hands in the terrifying rapidity of his gesticulations. They did not terrify Eva Denison. When Rattray took a step towards the speaker, with flashing eyes, it was some word from Eva that checked him; when Santos was done, it was to Rattray that she turned with her answer.

One instant I saw her very clearly, in the light of a candle.

I Live Again

"He calls me a liar for telling you that Mr. Cole knew all," said she, thrilling me with my own name. "Don't *you* say anything," she added, as the young man turned on Santos with a scowl; "you are one as wicked as the other, but there was a time when I thought differently of you: his character I have always known. Of the two evils, I prefer to speak to you."

Rattray bowed, humbly enough, I thought; but my darling's nostrils only curled the more.

"He calls me a liar," she continued; "so may you all. Since you have found it out, I admit it freely and without shame; one must be false in the hands of false fiends like all of you. Weakness is nothing to you; helplessness is nothing; you must be met with your own weapons, and so I lied in my sore extremity to gain the one miserable advantage within my reach. He says you found me out by making friends with Mr. Cole. He says that Mr. Cole has been dining with you in this very room, this very night. You still tell the truth sometimes; has that man—that demon—told it for once?"

"It is perfectly true," said Rattray in a low voice.

"And poor Mr. Cole told you that he knew nothing of your villany?"

Dead Men Tell No Tales

"I found out that he knew absolutely nothing
—after first thinking otherwise."

"Suppose he had known? What would you
have done?"

Rattray said nothing. Santos shrugged as he
lit a fresh cigarette. The captain went on with
his supper.

"Ashamed to say!" cried Eva Denison. "So
you have some shame left still! Well, I will tell
you. You would have murdered him, as you murdered all the rest; you would have killed him in
cold blood, as I wish and pray that you would
kill me!"

The young fellow faced her, white to the lips.
"You have no right to say that, Miss Denison!"
he cried. "I may be bad, but, as I am ready to
answer for my sins, the crime of murder is not
among them."

Well, it is still some satisfaction to remember
that my love never punished me with such a look
as was the young squire's reward for this protesta-
tion. The curl of the pink nostrils, the parting of
the proud lips, the gleam of the sound white teeth,
before a word was spoken, were more than I, for
one, could have borne. For I did not see the grief
underlying the scorn, but actually found it in my
heart to pity this poor devil of a Rattray: so hum-

bly fell those fine eyes of his, so like a dog did he stand, waiting to be whipped.

"Yes; you are very innocent!" she began at last, so softly that I could scarcely hear. "You have not committed murder, so you say; let it stand to your credit by all means. You have no blood upon your hands; you say so; that is enough. No! you are comparatively innocent, I admit. All you have done is to make murder easy for others; to get others to do the dirty work, and then shelter them and share the gain; all you need have on *your* conscience is every life that was lost with the *Lady Jermyn,* and every soul that lost itself in losing them. You call that innocence? Then give me honest guilt! Give me the man who set fire to the ship, and who sits there eating his supper; he is more of a man than you. Give me the wretch who has beaten men to death before my eyes; there's something great about a monster like that, there's something to loathe. His *assistant* is only little—mean—despicable!"

Loud and hurried in its wrath, low and deliberate in its contempt, all this was uttered with a furious and abnormal eloquence, which would have struck me, loving her, to the ground. On Rattray it had a different effect. His head lifted as she heaped abuse upon it, until he met her flashing eye with that of a man very thankful to take his deserts and something more; and to mine he was least despicable when that last word left her lips. When he saw that it was her last, he took her candle (she had put it down on the ancient settle against the door), and presented it to her with another bow. And so without a word he led her to the door, opened it, and bowed yet lower as she swept out, but still without a tinge of mockery in the obeisance.

He was closing the door after her when Joaquin Santos reached it.

"Diablo!" cried he. "Why let her go? We have not done with her."

"That doesn't matter; she is done with us," was the stern reply.

"It does matter," retorted Santos; "what is more, she is my step-daughter, and back she shall come!"

"She is also my visitor, and I'm damned if you're going to make her!"

An instant Santos stood, his back to me, his fingers working, his neck brown with blood; then his coat went into creases across the shoulders, and he was shrugging still as he turned away.

"Your veesitor!" said he. "Your veesitor! Your veesitor!"

I Live Again

Harris laughed outright as he raised his glass; the hot young squire had him by the collar, and the wine was spilling on the cloth, as I rose very cautiously and crept back to the path.

"When rogues fall out!" I was thinking to myself. "I shall save her yet—I shall save my darling!"

Already I was accustomed to the thought that she still lived, and to the big heart she had set beating in my feeble frame; already the continued existence of these villains, with the first dim inkling of their villainy, was ceasing to be a novelty in a brain now quickened and prehensile beyond belief. And yet—but a few minutes had I knelt at the window—but a few more was it since Rattray and I had shaken hands!

Not his visitor; his prisoner, without a doubt; but alive! alive! and neither guest nor prisoner for many hours more. O my love! O my heart's delight! Now I knew why I was spared; to save her; to snatch her from these rascals; to cherish and protect her evermore!

All the past shone clear behind me; the dark was lightness and the crooked straight. All the future lay clear ahead; it presented no difficulties yet; a mad, ecstatic confidence was mine for the wildest, happiest moments of my life.

Dead Men Tell No Tales

I stood upright in the darkness. I saw her light!

It was ascending the tower at the building's end; now in this window it glimmered, now in the one above. At last it was steady, high up near the stars, and I stole below.

"Eva! Eva!"

There was no answer. Low as it was, my voice was alarming; it cooled and cautioned me. I sought little stones. I crept back to throw them. Ah God! her form eclipsed that lighted slit in the gray stone tower. I heard her weeping high above me at her window.

"Eva! Eva!"

There was a pause, and then a little cry of gladness.

"Is it Mr. Cole?" came in an eager whisper through her tears.

"Yes! yes! I was outside the window. I heard everything——"

"*They* will hear *you!*" she cried softly, in a steadier voice.

"No—listen!" They were quarrelling. Rattray's voice was loud and angry. "They cannot hear," I continued, in more cautious tones; "they think I'm in bed and asleep half-a-mile away. Oh, thank God! I'll get you away from them; trust me, my love, my darling!"

I Live Again

In my madness I knew not what I said; it was my wild heart speaking. Some moments passed before she replied.

"Will you promise to do nothing I ask you not to do?"

"Of course."

"My life might answer for it——"

"I promise—I promise."

"Then wait—hide—watch my light. When you see it back in the window, watch with all your eyes! I am going to write and then throw it out. Not another syllable!"

She was gone; there was a long yellow slit in the masonry once more; her light burnt faint and far within.

I retreated among some bushes and kept watch.

The moon was skimming beneath the surface of a sea of clouds: now the black billows had silver crests: now an incandescent buoy bobbed among them. O for enough light, and no more!

In the hall the high voices were more subdued. I heard the captain's tipsy laugh. My eyes fastened themselves upon that faint and lofty light, and on my heels I crouched among the bushes.

The flame moved, flickered, and shone small

but brilliant on the very sill. I ran forward on tip-toe. A white flake fluttered to my feet. I secured it and waited for one word; none came; but the window was softly shut.

I stood in doubt, the treacherous moonlight all over me now, and once more the window opened.

"Go quickly!"

And again it was shut; next moment I was stealing close by the spot where I had knelt. I saw within once more.

Harris nodded in his chair. The nigger had disappeared. Rattray was lighting a candle, and the Portuguese holding out his hand for the match.

"Did you lock the gate, senhor?" asked Santos.

"No; but I will now."

As I opened it I heard a door open within. I could hardly let the latch down again for the sudden trembling of my fingers. The key turned behind me ere I had twenty yards' start.

Thank God there was light enough now! I followed the beck. I found my way. I stood in the open valley, between the oak-plantation and my desolate cottage, and I kissed my tiny, twisted note again and again in a paroxysm of passion and of insensate joy. Then I unfolded it and held it to my eyes in the keen October moonshine.

CHAPTER XII

MY LADY'S BIDDING

SCRIBBLED in sore haste, by a very tremulous little hand, with a pencil, on the flyleaf of some book, my darling's message is still difficult to read; it was doubly so in the moonlight, five-and-forty autumns ago. My eyesight, however, was then perhaps the soundest thing about me, and in a little I had deciphered enough to guess correctly (as it proved) at the whole:—

"You say you heard everything just now, and there is no time for further explanations. I am in the hands of villains, but not ill-treated, though they are one as bad as the other. You will not find it easy to rescue me. I don't see how it is to be done. You have promised not to do anything I ask you not to do, and I *implore you not to tell a soul* until you have seen *me* again and heard more. *You might just as well kill me as come back now with help.*

"You see you know nothing, though I told them you knew all. And so you shall as soon as I can see you for five minutes face to face. In the meantime do *nothing*—know nothing when you see Mr. Rattray—unless you wish to be my death.

129

Dead Men Tell No Tales

"It would have been possible last night, and it may be again to-morrow night. They all go out every night when they can, except José, who is left in charge. They are out from nine or ten till two or three; if they are out to-morrow night my candle will be close to the window as I shall put it when I have finished this. You can see my window from over the wall. If the light is in front you must climb the wall, for they will leave the gate locked. I shall see you and will bribe José to let me out for a turn. He has done it before for a bottle of wine. I can manage him. Can I trust to you? If you break your promise—but you will not? One of them would as soon kill me as smoke a cigarette, and the rest are under his thumb. I dare not write more. But *my life* is in your hands.

"Eva Denison."

"Oh! beware of the woman Braithwaite; she is about the worst of the gang."

I could have burst out crying in my bitter discomfiture, mortification, and alarm: to think that her life was in my hands, and that it depended, not on that prompt action which was the one course I had contemplated, but on twenty-four hours of resolute inactivity!

I would not think it. I refused the condition. It took away my one prop, my one stay, that prospect of immediate measures which alone preserved in me such coolness as I had retained until now. I was cool no longer; where I had relied on prac-

My Lady's Bidding

tical direction I was baffled and hindered and driven mad; on my honor I believe I was little less for some moments, groaning, cursing, and beating the air with impotent fists—in one of them my poor love's letter crushed already to a ball.

Danger and difficulty I had been prepared to face; but the task that I was set was a hundredfold harder than any that had whirled through my teeming brain. To sit still; to do nothing; to pretend I knew nothing; an hour of it would destroy my reason—and I was invited to wait twenty-four!

No; my word was passed; keep it I must. She knew the men, she must know best; and her life depended on my obedience: she made that so plain. Obey I must and would; to make a start, I tottered over the plank that spanned the beck, and soon I saw the cottage against the moonlit sky. I came up to it. I drew back in sudden fear. It was alight upstairs and down, and the gaunt strong figure of the woman Braithwaite stood out as I had seen it first, in the doorway, with the light showing warmly through her rank red hair.

"Is that you, Mr. Cole?" she cried in a tone that she reserved for me; yet through the forced amiability there rang a note of genuine surprise.

She had been prepared for me never to return at all!

My knees gave under me as I forced myself to advance; but my wits took new life from the crisis, and in a flash I saw how to turn my weakness into account. I made a false step on my way to the door; when I reached it I leant heavily against the jam, and I said with a slur that I felt unwell. I had certainly been flushed with wine when I left Rattray; it would be no bad thing for him to hear that I had arrived quite tipsy at the cottage; should he discover I had been near an hour on the way, here was my explanation cut and dried.

So I shammed a degree of intoxication with apparent success, and Jane Braithwaite gave me her arm up the stairs. My God, how strong it was, and how weak was mine!

Left to myself, I reeled about my bedroom, pretending to undress; then out with my candles, and into bed in all my clothes, until the cottage should be quiet. Yes, I must lie still and feign sleep, with every nerve and fibre leaping within me, lest the she-devil below should suspect me of suspicions! It was with her I had to cope for the next four-and-twenty hours; and she filled me with a greater present terror than all those villains at

My Lady's Bidding

the hall; for had not their poor little helpless captive described her as "about the worst of the gang?"

To think that my love lay helpless there in the hands of those wretches; and to think that her lover lay helpless here in the supervision of this vile virago!

It must have been one or two in the morning when I stole to my sitting-room window, opened it, and sat down to think steadily, with the counterpane about my shoulders.

The moon sailed high and almost full above the clouds; these were dispersing as the night wore on, and such as remained were of a beautiful soft tint between white and gray. The sky was too light for stars, and beneath it the open country stretched so clear and far that it was as though one looked out at noonday through slate-colored glass. Down the dewy slope below my window a few calves fed with toothless mouthings; the beck was very audible, the oak-trees less so; but for these peaceful sounds the stillness and the solitude were equally intense.

I may have sat there like a mouse for half an hour. The reason was that I had become mercifully engrossed in one of the subsidiary problems: whether it would be better to drop from the window or to trust to the creaking stairs. Would the creaking be much worse than the thud, and the difference worth the risk of a sprained ankle? Well worth it, I at length decided; the risk was nothing; my window was scarce a dozen feet from the ground. How easily it could be done, how quickly, how safely in this deep stillness and bright moonlight! I would fall so lightly on my stocking soles; a single soft, dull thud; then away under the moon without fear or risk of a false step; away over the stone walls to the main road, and so to the nearest police-station with my tale; and before sunrise the villains would be taken in their beds, and my darling would be safe!

I sprang up softly. Why not do it now? Was I bound to keep my rash, blind promise? Was it possible these murderers would murder her? I struck a match on my trousers, I lit a candle, I read her letter carefully again, and again it maddened and distracted me. I struck my hands together. I paced the room wildly. Caution deserted me, and I made noise enough to wake the very mute; lost to every consideration but that of the terrifying day before me, the day of silence and of inactivity, that I must live through with an unsuspecting face, a cool head, a civil tongue! The prospect appalled me as nothing else could

My Lady's Bidding

or did; nay, the sudden noise upon the stairs, the knock at my door, and the sense that I had betrayed myself already—that even now all was over—these came as a relief after the haunting terror which they interrupted.

I flung the door open, and there stood Mrs. Braithwaite, as fully dressed as myself.

"You'll not be very well, sir?"

"No, I'm not."

"What's t' matter wi' you?"

This second question was rude and fierce with suspicion: the real woman rang out in it, yet its effect on me was astonishing: once again was I inspired to turn my slip into a move.

"Matter?" I cried. "Can't you see what's the matter; couldn't you see when I came in? Drink's the matter! I came in drunk, and now I'm mad. I can't stand it; I'm not in a fit state. Do you know nothing of me? Have they told you nothing? I'm the only man that was saved from the *Lady Jermyn*, the ship that was burned to the water's edge with every soul but me. My nerves are in little ends. I came down here for peace and quiet and sleep. Do you know that I have hardly slept for two months? And now I shall never sleep again! O my God I shall die for want of it! The wine has done it. I never should have touched a drop. I can't stand it; I can't sleep after it; I shall kill myself if I get no sleep. Do you hear, you woman? I shall kill myself in your house if I don't get to sleep!"

I saw her shrink, virago as she was. I waved my arms, I shrieked in her face. It was not all acting. Heaven knows how true it was about the sleep. I was slowly dying of insomnia. I was a nervous wreck. She must have heard it. Now she saw it for herself.

No; it was by no means all acting. Intending only to lie, I found myself telling little but the strictest truth, and longing for sleep as passionately as though I had nothing to keep me awake. And yet, while my heart cried aloud in spite of me, and my nerves relieved themselves in this unpremeditated ebullition, I was all the time watching its effect as closely as though no word of it had been sincere.

Mrs. Braithwaite seemed frightened; not at all pitiful; and as I calmed down she recovered her courage and became insolent. I had spoilt her night. She had not been told she was to take in a raving lunatic. She would speak to Squire Rattray in the morning.

"Morning?" I yelled after her as she went. "Send your husband to the nearest chemist as soon as it's dawn; send him for chloral, chloroform, morphia, anything they've got and as much of it as they'll let him have. I'll give you five pounds if you get me what'll send me to sleep all to-morrow—and to-morrow night!"

Never, I feel sure, were truth and falsehood more craftily interwoven; yet I had thought of none of it until the woman was at my door, while of much I had not thought at all: It had rushed from my heart and from my lips. And no sooner was I alone than I burst into hysterical tears, only to stop and compliment myself because they sounded genuine—as though they were not! Towards morning I took to my bed in a burning fever, and lay there, now congratulating myself upon it, because when night came they would all think me so secure; and now weeping because the night might find me dying or dead. So I tossed, with her note clasped in my hand underneath the sheets; and beneath my very body that stout weapon that I had bought in town. I might not have to use it, but I was fatalist enough to fancy that I should. In the meantime it helped me to lie still, my thoughts fixed on the night, and the day made easy for me after all.

If only I could sleep!

About nine o'clock Jane Braithwaite paid me

a surly visit; in half an hour she was back with tea and toast and an altered mien. She not only lit my fire, but treated me the while to her original tone of almost fervent civility and respect and determination. Her vagaries soon ceased to puzzle me: the psychology of Jane Braithwaite was not recondite. In the night it had dawned upon her that Rattray had found me harmless and was done with me, therefore there was no need for her to put herself out any further on my account. In the morning, finding me really ill, she had gone to the hall in alarm; her subsequent attentions were an act of obedience; and in their midst came Rattray himself to my bedside.

CHAPTER XIII

THE LONGEST DAY OF MY LIFE

THE boy looked so blithe and buoyant, so gallant and still so frank, that even now I could not think as meanly of him as poor Eva did. A rogue he must be, but surely not the petty rogue that she had made him out. Yet it was dirty work that he had done by me; and there I had to lie and take his kind, false, felon's hand in mine.

"My poor dear fellow," he cried, "I'm most sorry to find you like this. But I was afraid of it last night. It's all this infernally strong air!"

How I longed to tell him what it was, and to see his face! The thought of Eva alone restrained me, and I retorted as before, in a tone I strove to make as friendly, that it was his admirable wine and nothing else.

"But you took hardly any."

"I shouldn't have touched a drop. I can't stand it. Instead of soothing me it excites me to the verge of madness. I'm almost over the verge—for want of sleep—my trouble ever since *the* trouble."

Dead Men Tell No Tales

Again I was speaking the literal truth, and again congratulating myself as though it were a lie: the fellow looked so distressed at my state; indeed I believe that his distress was as genuine as mine, and his sentiments as involved. He took my hand again, and his brow wrinkled at its heat. He asked for the other hand to feel my pulse. I had to drop my letter to comply.

"I wish to goodness there was something I could do for you," he said. "Would you—would you care to see a doctor?"

I shook my head, and could have smiled at his visible relief.

"Then I'm going to prescribe for you," he said with decision. "It's the place that doesn't agree with you, and it was I who brought you to the place; therefore it's for me to get you out of it as quick as possible. Up you get, and I'll drive you to the station myself!"

I had another work to keep from smiling: he was so ingenuously disingenuous. There was less to smile at in his really nervous anxiety to get me away. I lay there reading him like a book: it was not my health that concerned him, of course: was it my safety? I told him he little knew how ill I was—an inglorious speech that came hard, though not by any means untrue. "Move me with this

The Longest Day of My Life

fever on me?" said I; "it would be as much as my miserable life is worth.",

"I'm afraid," said he, "that it may be as much as your life's worth to stay on here!" And there was such real fear, in his voice and eyes, that it reconciled me there and then to the discomfort of a big revolver between the mattress and the small of my back. "We must get you out of it," he continued, "the moment you feel fit to stir. Shall we say to-morrow?"

"If you like," I said, advisedly; "and if I can get some sleep to-day."

"Then to-morrow it is! You see I *know* it's the climate," he added, jumping from tone to tone; "it *couldn't* have been those two or three glasses of sound wine."

"Shall I tell you what it is?" I said, looking him full in the face, with eyes that I dare say were wild enough with fever and insomnia. "It's the burning of the *Lady Jermyn!*" I cried. "It's the faces and the shrieks of the women; it's the cursing and the fighting of the men; it's boat-loads struggling in an oily sea; it's husbands and wives jumping overboard together; it's men turned into devils, it's hell-fire afloat——"

"Stop! stop!" he whispered, hoarse as a crow. I was sitting up with my hot eyes upon him. He was white as the quilt, and the bed shook with his trembling. I had gone as far as was prudent, and I lay back with a glow of secret satisfaction.

"Yes, I will stop," said I, "and I wouldn't have begun if you hadn't found it so difficult to understand my trouble. Now you know what it is. It's the old trouble. I came up here to forget it; instead of that I drink too much and tell you all about it; and the two things together have bowled me over. But I'll go to-morrow; only give me something to put me asleep till then."

"I will!" he vowed. "I'll go myself to the nearest chemist, and he shall give me the very strongest stuff he's got. Good-by, and don't you stir till I come back—for your own sake. I'll go this minute, and I'll ride like hell!" And if ever two men were glad to be rid of each other, they were this young villain and myself.

But what was his villany? It was little enough that I had overheard at the window, and still less that poor Eva had told me in her hurried lines. All I saw clearly was that the *Lady Jermyn* and some hundred souls had perished by the foulest of foul play; that, besides Eva and myself, only the incendiaries had escaped; that somehow these wretches had made a second escape from the gig, leaving dead men and word of their own death be-

The Longest Day of My Life

hind them in the boat. And here the motive was as much a mystery to me as the means; but, in my present state, both were also matters of supreme indifference. My one desire was to rescue my love from her loathsome captors; of little else did I pause to think. Yet Rattray's visit left its own mark on my mind; and long after he was gone I lay puzzling over the connection between a young Lancastrian, of good name, of ancient property, of great personal charm, and a crime of unparalleled atrocity committed in cold blood on the high seas. That his complicity was flagrant I had no room to doubt, after Eva's own indictment of him, uttered to his face and in my hearing. Was it then the usual fraud on the underwriters, and was Rattray the inevitable accomplice on dry land? I could think of none but the conventional motive for destroying a vessel. Yet I knew there must be another and a subtler one, to account not only for the magnitude of the crime, but for the pains which the actual perpetrators had taken to conceal the fact of their survival, and for the union of so diverse a trinity as Senhor Santos, Captain Harris, and the young squire.

It must have been about mid-day when Rattray reappeared, ruddy, spurred, and splashed with mud; a comfort to sick eyes, I declare, in spite of all. He brought me two little vials, put one on the chimney-piece, poured the other into my tumbler, and added a little water.

"There, old fellow," said he; "swallow that, and if you don't get some sleep the chemist who made it up is the greatest liar unhung."

"What is it?' I asked, the glass in my hand, and my eyes on those of my companion.

"I don't know," said he. "I just told them to make up the strongest sleeping-draught that was safe, and I mentioned something about your case. Toss it off, man; it's sure to be all right."

Yes, I could trust him; he was not that sort of villain, for all that Eva Denison had said. I liked his face as well as ever. I liked his eye, and could have sworn to its honesty as I drained the glass. Even had it been otherwise, I must have taken my chance or shown him all; as it was, when he had pulled down my blind, and shaken my pillow, and he gave me his hand once more, I took it with involuntary cordiality. I only grieved that so fine a young fellow should have involved himself in so villainous a business; yet for Eva's sake I was glad that he had; for my mind failed (rather than refused) to believe him so black as she had painted him.

The long, long afternoon that followed I never

The Longest Day of My Life

shall forget. The opiate racked my head; it did not do its work; and I longed to sleep till evening with a longing I have never known before or since. Everything seemed to depend upon it; I should be a man again, if only I could first be a log for a few hours. But no; my troubles never left me for an instant; and there I must lie, pretending that they had! For the other draught was for the night; and if they but thought the first one had taken due effect, so much the less would they trouble their heads about me when they believed that I had swallowed the second.

Oh, but it was cruel! I lay and wept with weakness and want of sleep; ere night fell I knew that it would find me useless, if indeed my reason lingered on. To lie there helpless when Eva was expecting me, that would be the finishing touch. I should rise a maniac if ever I rose at all. More probably I would put one of my five big bullets into my own splitting head; it was no small temptation, lying there in a double agony, with the loaded weapon by my side.

Then sometimes I thought it was coming; and perhaps for an instant I would be tossing in my hen-coop; then back once more. And I swear that my physical and mental torments, here in my bed, would have been incomparably greater than anything I had endured on the sea, but for the saving grace of one sweet thought. She lived! She lived! And the God who had taken care of me, a castaway, would surely deliver her also from the hands of murderers and thieves. But not through me—I lay weak and helpless—and my tears ran again and yet again as I felt myself growing hourly weaker.

I remember what a bright fine day it was, with the grand open country all smiles beneath a clear, almost frosty sky, once when I got up on tip-toe and peeped out. A keen wind whistled about the cottage; I felt it on my feet as I stood; but never have I known a more perfect and invigorating autumn day. And there I must lie, with the manhood ebbing out of me, the manhood that I needed so for the night! I crept back into bed. I swore that I would sleep. Yet there I lay, listening sometimes to that vile woman's tread below; sometimes to mysterious whispers, between whom I neither knew nor cared; anon to my watch ticking by my side, to the heart beating in my body, hour after hour—hour after hour. I prayed as I have seldom prayed. I wept as I have never wept. I railed and blasphemed—not with my lips, because the woman must think I was asleep— but so much the more viciously in my heart.

The Longest Day of My Life

Suddenly it turned dark. There were no gradations—not even a tropical twilight. One minute I saw the sun upon the blind; the next—thank God! Oh, thank God! No light broke any longer through the blind; just a faint and narrow glimmer stole between it and the casement; and the light that had been bright golden was palest silver now.

It was the moon. I had been in dreamless sleep for hours.

The joy of that discovery! The transport of waking to it, and waking refreshed! The swift and sudden miracle that it seemed! I shall never, never forget it, still less the sickening thrill of fear which was cruelly quick to follow upon my joy. The cottage was still as the tomb. What if I had slept too long!

With trembling hand I found my watch. Luckily I had wound it in the early morning. I now carried it to the window, drew back the blind, and held it in the moonlight. It was not quite ten o'clock. And yet the cottage was so still—so still.

I stole to the door, opened it by cautious degrees, and saw the reflection of a light below. Still not a sound could I hear, save the rapid drawing of my own breath, and the startled beating of my own heart.

Dead Men Tell No Tales

I now felt certain that the Braithwaites were out, and dressed hastily, making as little noise as possible, and still hearing absolutely none from below. Then, feeling faint with hunger, though a new being after my sleep, I remembered a packet of sandwiches which I had not opened on my journey north. These I transferred from my travelling-bag (where they had lain forgotten) to my pocket, before drawing down the blind, leaving the room on tip-toe, and very gently fastening the door behind me. On the stairs, too, I trod with the utmost caution, feeling the wall with my left hand (my right was full), lest by any chance I might be mistaken in supposing I had the cottage to myself. In spite of my caution there came a creak at every step. And to my sudden horror I heard a chair move in the kitchen below.

My heart and I stood still together. But my right hand tightened on stout wood, my right forefinger trembled against thin steel. The sound was not repeated. And at length I continued on my way down, my teeth set, an excuse on my lips, but determination in every fibre of my frame.

A shadow lay across the kitchen floor; it was that of the deaf mute, as he stood on a chair before the fire, supporting himself on the chimney-

The Longest Day of My Life

piece with one puny arm, while he reached overhead with the other. I stood by for an instant,
glorying in the thought that he could not hear me;
the next, I saw what it was he was reaching up
for—a bell-mouthed blunderbuss—and I knew
the little devil for the impostor that he was.

"You touch it," said I, "and you'll drop dead
on that hearth."

He pretended not to hear me, but he heard the
click of the splendid spring which Messrs. Deane
and Adams had put into that early revolver of
theirs, and he could not have come down much
quicker with my bullet in his spine.

"Now, then," I said, "what the devil do you
mean by shamming deaf and dumb?"

"I niver said I was owt o' t' sort," he whimpered, cowering behind the chair in a sullen
ague.

"But you acted it, and I've a jolly good mind
to shoot you dead!" (Remember, I was so weak
myself that I thought my arm would break from
presenting my five chambers and my ten-inch barrel; otherwise I should be sorry to relate how I
bullied that mouse of a man.) "I may let you
off," I continued, "if you answer questions.
Where's your wife?"

"Eh, she'll be back directly!" said Braithwaite,

149

with some tact; but his look was too cunning to give the warning weight.

"I've a bullet to spare for her," said I, cheerfully; "now, then, where is she?"

"Gone wi' the oothers, for owt I knaw."

"And where are the others gone?"

"Where they allus go, ower to t' say."

"Over to the sea, eh? We're getting on! What takes them there?"

"That's more than I can tell you, sir," said Braithwaite, with so much emphasis and so little reluctance as to convince me that for once at least he had spoken the truth. There was even a spice of malice in his tone. I began to see possibilities in the little beast.

"Well," I said, "you're a nice lot! I don't know what your game is, and don't want to. I've had enough of you without that. I'm off to-night."

"Before they get back?" asked Braithwaite, plainly in doubt about his duty, and yet as plainly relieved to learn the extent of my intention.

"Certainly," said I; "why not? I'm not particularly anxious to see your wife again, and you may ask Mr. Rattray from me why the devil he led me to suppose you were deaf and dumb? Or, if you like, you needn't say anything at all about it," I added, seeing his thin jaw fall; "tell him I never found you out, but just felt well enough to go, and went. When do you expect them back?"

"It won't be yet a bit," said he.

"Good! Now look here. What would you say to these?" And I showed him a couple of sovereigns: I longed to offer him twenty, but feared to excite his suspicions. "These are yours if you have a conveyance at the end of the lane— the lane we came up the night before last—in an hour's time."

His dull eyes glistened; but a tremor took him from top to toe, and he shook his head.

"I'm ill, man!" I cried. "If I stay here I'll die! Mr. Rattray knows that, and he wanted me to go this morning; he'll be only too thankful to find me gone."

This argument appealed to him; indeed, I was proud of it.

"But I was to stop an' look after you," he mumbled; "it'll get me into trooble, it will that!"

I took out three more sovereigns; not a penny higher durst I go.

"Will five pounds repay you? No need to tell your wife it was five, you know! I should keep four of them all to myself."

The cupidity of the little wretch was at last

Dead Men Tell No Tales

overcoming his abject cowardice. I could see him making up his miserable mind. And I still flatter myself that I took only safe (and really cunning) steps to precipitate the process. To offer him more money would have been madness; instead, I poured it all back into my pocket.

"All right!" I cried; "you're a greedy, cowardly, old idiot, and I'll just save my money." And out I marched into the moonlight, very briskly, towards the lane; he was so quick to follow me that I had no fears of the blunderbuss, but quickened my step, and soon had him running at my heels.

"Stop, stop, sir! You're that hasty wi' a poor owd man." So he whimpered as he followed me like the little cur he was.

"I'm hanged if I stop," I answered without looking back; and had him almost in tears before I swung round on him so suddenly that he yelped with fear. "What are you bothering me for?" I blustered. "Do you want me to wring your neck?"

"Oh, I'll go, sir! I'll go, I'll go," he moaned.

"I've a good mind not to let you. I wouldn't if I was fit to walk five miles."

"But I'll roon 'em, sir! I will that! I'll go as fast as iver I can!"

152

The Longest Day of My Life

"And have a conveyance at the road-end of the lane as near an hour hence as you possibly can?"

"Why, there, sir!" he cried, crassly inspired; "I could drive you in our own trap in half the time."

"Oh, no, you couldn't! I—I'm not fit to be out at all; it must be a closed conveyance; but I'll come to the end of the lane to save time, so let him wait there. You needn't wait yourself; here's a sovereign of your money, and I'll leave the rest in the jug in my bedroom. There! It's worth your while to trust me, I think. As for my luggage, I'll write to Mr. Rattray about that. But I'll be shot if I spend another night on his property."

I was rid of him at last; and there I stood, listening to his headlong steps, until they stumbled out of earshot down the lane; then back to the cottage, at a run myself, and up to my room to be no worse than my word. The sovereigns plopped into the water and rang together at the bottom of the jug. In another minute I was hastening through the plantation, in my hand the revolver that had served me well already, and was still loaded and capped in all five chambers.

CHAPTER XIV

IN THE GARDEN

IT so happened that I met nobody at all; but I must confess that my luck was better than my management. As I came upon the beck, a new sound reached me with the swirl. It was the jingle of bit and bridle; the beat of hoofs came after; and I had barely time to fling myself flat, when two horsemen emerged from the plantation, riding straight towards me in the moonlight. If they continued on that course they could not fail to see me as they passed along the opposite bank. However, to my unspeakable relief, they were scarce clear of the trees when they turned their horses' heads, rode them through the water a good seventy yards from where I lay, and so away at a canter across country towards the road. On my hands and knees I had a good look at them as they bobbed up and down under the moon; and my fears subsided in astonished curiosity. For I have already boasted of my eyesight, and I could have sworn that neither Rattray nor any one of his guests was of the horsemen; yet the

In the Garden

back and shoulders of one of these seemed somehow familiar to me. Not that I wasted many
moments over the coincidence, for I had other
things to think about as I ran on to the hall.

I found the rear of the building in darkness
unrelieved from within; on the other hand, the
climbing moon beat so full upon the garden wall,
it was as though a lantern pinned me as I crept
beneath it. In passing I thought I might as well
try the gate; but Eva was right; it was locked;
and that made me half inclined to distrust my eyes
in the matter of the two horsemen, for whence
could they have come, if not from the hall? In
any case I was well rid of them. I now followed
the wall some little distance, and then, to see
over it, walked backwards until I was all but in
the beck; and there, sure enough, shone my darling's candle, close as close against the diamond
panes of her narrow, lofty window! It brought
those ready tears back to my foolish, fevered eyes.
But for sentiment there was no time, and every
other emotion was either futile or premature. So
I mastered my full heart, I steeled my wretched
nerves, and braced my limp muscles for the task
that lay before them.

I had a garden wall to scale, nearly twice my
own height, and without notch or cranny in the

ancient, solid masonry. I stood against it on my toes, and I touched it with my finger-tips as high up as possible. Some four feet severed them from the coping that left only half a sky above my upturned eyes.

I do not know whether I have made it plain that the house was not surrounded by four walls, but merely filled a breach in one of the four, which nipped it (as it were) at either end. The back entrance was approachable enough, but barred or watched, I might be very sure. It is ever the vulnerable points which are most securely guarded, and it was my one comfort that the difficult way must also be the safe way, if only the difficulty could be overcome. How to overcome it was the problem. I followed the wall right round to the point at which it abutted on the tower that immured my love; the height never varied; nor could my hands or eyes discover a single foot-hole, ledge, or other means of mounting to the top.

Yet my hot head was full of ideas; and I wasted some minutes in trying to lift from its hinges a solid, six-barred, outlying gate, that my weak arms could hardly stir. More time went in pulling branches from the oak-trees about the beck, where the latter ran nearest to the moonlit

In the Garden

wall. I had an insane dream of throwing a long forked branch over the coping, and so swarming up hand-over-hand. But even to me the impracticability of this plan came home at last. And there I stood in a breathless lather, much time and strength thrown away together; and the candle burning down for nothing in that little lofty window; and the running water swirling noisily over its stones at my back.

This was the only sound; the wind had died away; the moonlit valley lay as still as the dread old house in its midst but for the splash and gurgle of the beck. I fancied this grew louder as I paused and listened in my helplessness. All at once—was it the tongue of Nature telling me the way, or common gumption returning at the eleventh hour? I ran down to the water's edge, and could have shouted for joy. Great stones lay in equal profusion on bed and banks. I lifted one of the heaviest in both hands. I staggered with it to the wall. I came back for another; for some twenty minutes I was so employed; my ultimate reward a fine heap of boulders against the wall.

Then I began to build; then mounted my pile, clawing the wall to keep my balance. My fingers were still many inches from the coping. I jumped

down and gave another ten minutes to the back-
breaking work of carrying more boulders from
the water to the wall. Then I widened my cairn
below, so that I could stand firmly before spring-
ing upon the pinnacle with which I completed it.
I knew well that this would collapse under me
if I allowed my weight to rest more than an
instant upon it. And so at last it did; but my fingers had clutched the coping in time; had grabbed
it even as the insecure pyramid crumbled and left
me dangling.

Instantly exerting what muscle I had left, and
the occasion gave me, I succeeded in pulling myself up until my chin was on a level with my
hands, when I flung an arm over and caught the
inner coping. The other arm followed; then a
leg; and at last I sat astride the wall, panting and
palpitating, and hardly able to credit my own
achievement. One great difficulty had been my
huge revolver. I had been terribly frightened it
might go off, and had finally used my cravat to
sling it at the back of my neck. It had shifted a
little, and I was working it round again, prepara-
tory to my drop, when I saw the light suddenly
taken from the window in the tower, and a ker-
chief waving for one instant in its place. So she
had been waiting and watching for me all these

In the Garden

hours! I dropped into the garden in a very ecstasy of grief and rapture, to think that I had been so long in coming to my love, but that I had come at last. And I picked myself up in a very frenzy of fear lest, after all, I should fail to spirit her from this horrible place.

Doubly desolate it looked in the rays of that bright October moon. Skulking in the shadow of the wall which had so long baffled me, I looked across a sharp border of shade upon a chaos, the more striking for its lingering trim design. The long, straight paths were barnacled with weeds; the dense, fine hedges, once prim and angular, had fattened out of all shape or form; and on the velvet sward of other days you might have waded waist high in rotten hay. Towards the garden end this rank jungle merged into a worse wilderness of rhododendrons, the tallest I have ever seen. On all this the white moon smiled, and the grim house glowered, to the eternal swirl and rattle of the beck beyond its walls.

Long enough I stood where I had dropped, listening with all my being for some other sound; but at last that great studded door creaked and shivered on its ancient hinges, and I heard voices arguing in the Portuguese tongue. It was poor Eva wheedling that black rascal José. I saw her in the lighted porch; the nigger I saw also, shrugging and gesticulating for all the world like his hateful master; yet giving in, I felt certain, though I could not understand a word that reached me.

And indeed my little mistress very soon sailed calmly out, followed by final warnings and expostulations hurled from the step: for the black stood watching her as she came steadily my way, now raising her head to sniff the air, now stooping to pluck up a weed, the very picture of a prisoner seeking the open air for its own sake solely. I had a keen eye apiece for them as I cowered closer to the wall, revolver in hand. But ere my love was very near me (for she would stand long moments gazing ever so innocently at the moon), her jailer had held a bottle to the light, and had beaten a retreat so sudden and so hasty that I expected him back every moment, and so durst not stir. Eva saw me, however, and contrived to tell me so without interrupting the air that she was humming as she walked.

"Follow me," she sang, "only keep as you are, keep as you are, close to the wall, close to the wall."

And on she strolled to her own tune, and came abreast of me without turning her head; so I

crept in the shadow (my ugly weapon tucked out
of sight), and she sauntered in the shine, until we
came to the end of the garden, where the path
turned at right angles, running behind the rhododendrons; once in their shelter, she halted and
beckoned me, and next instant I had her hands
in mine.

"At last!" was all that I could say for many
a moment, as I stood there gazing into her dear
eyes, no hero in my heroic hour, but the bigger
love-sick fool than ever. "But quick—quick—
quick!" I added, as she brought me to my senses
by withdrawing her hands. "We've no time to
lose." And I looked wildly from wall to wall,
only to find them as barren and inaccessible on this
side as on the other.

"We have more time than you think," were
Eva's first words. "We can do nothing for half-
an-hour."

"Why not?"

"I'll tell you in a minute. How did you manage to get over?"

"Brought boulders from the beck, and piled
'em up till I could reach the top."

I thought her eyes glistened.

"What patience!" she cried softly. "We must
find a simpler way of getting out—and I think

I have. They've all gone, you know, but José."

"All three?"

"The captain has been gone all day."

Then the other two must have been my horsemen, very probably in some disguise; and my head swam with the thought of the risk that I had run at the very moment when I thought myself safest. Well, I would have finished them both! But I did not say so to Eva. I did not mention the incident, I was so fearful of destroying her confidence in me. Apologizing, therefore, for my interruption, without explaining it, I begged her to let me hear her plan.

It was simple enough. There was no fear of the others returning before midnight; the chances were that they would be very much later; and now it was barely eleven, and Eva had promised not to stay out above half-an-hour. When it was up José would come and call her.

"It is horrid to have to be so cunning!" cried little Eva, with an angry shudder; "but it's no use thinking of that," she was quick enough to add, "when you have such dreadful men to deal with, such fiends! And I have had all day to prepare, and have suffered till I am so desperate I would rather die to-night than spend another in that

In the Garden

house. No; let me finish! José will come round here to look for me. But you and I will be hiding on the other side of these rhododendrons. And when we hear him here we'll make a dash for it across the long grass. Once let us get the door shut and locked in his face, and he'll be in a trap. It will take him some time to break in; time enough to give us a start; what's more, when he finds us gone, he'll do what they all used to do in any doubt."

"What's that?"

"Say nothing till it's found out; then lie for their lives; and it *was* their lives, poor creatures on the Zambesi!" She was silent a moment, her determined little face hard-set upon some unforgotten horror. "Once we get away, I shall be surprised if it's found out till morning," concluded Eva, without a word as to what I was to do with her; neither, indeed, had I myself given that question a moment's consideration.

"Then let's make a dash for it now!" was all I said or thought.

"No; they can't come yet, and José is strong and brutal, and I have heard how ill you are. That you should have come to me notwithstanding——" and she broke off with her little hands lying so gratefully on my shoulders, that I know not how I refrained from catching her then and there to my heart. Instead, I laughed and said that my illness was a pure and deliberate sham, and my presence there its direct result. And such was the virtue in my beloved's voice, the magic of her eyes, the healing of her touch, that I was scarce conscious of deceit, but felt a whole man once more as we two stood together in the moonlight.

In a trance I stood there gazing into her brave young eyes. In a trance I suffered her to lead me by the hand through the rank, dense rhododendrons. And still entranced I crouched by her side near the further side, with only unkempt grassplot and a weedy path between us and that ponderous door, wide open still, and replaced by a section of the lighted hall within. On this we fixed our attention with mingled dread, and impatience, those contending elements of suspense; but the black was slow to reappear; and my eyes stole home to my sweet girl's face, with its glory of moonlit curls, and the eager, resolute, embittered look that put the world back two whole months, and Eva Denison upon the *Lady Jermyn's* poop, in the ship's last hours. But it was not her look alone; she had on her cloak, as the night before, but with me (God bless her!)

In the Garden

she found no need to clasp herself in its folds;
and underneath she wore the very dress in which
she had sung at our last concert, and been rescued
in the gig. It looked as though she had worn it
ever since. The roses were crushed and soiled,
the tulle all torn, and tarnished some strings of
beads that had been gold: a tatter of Chantilly lace
hung by a thread: it is another of the relics that I
have unearthed in the writing of this narrative.

"I thought men never noticed dresses?" my
love said suddenly, a pleased light in her eyes (I
thought) in spite of all. "Do you really remember it?"

"I remember every one of them," I said indig-
nantly; and so I did.

"You will wonder why I wear it," said Eva,
quickly. "It was the first that came that terrible
night. They have given me many since. But I
won't wear one of them—not one!"

- How her eyes flashed! I forgot all about José.

"I suppose you know why they hadn't room
for you in the gig?" she went on.

"No, I don't know, and I don't care. They
had room for *you*," said I; "that's all I care
about." And to think she could not see I loved her!

"But do you mean to say you don't know that
these—murderers—set fire to the ship?"

Dead Men Tell No Tales

"No—yes! I heard you say so last night."

"And you don't want to know what for?"

Out of politeness I protested that I did; but, as I live, all I wanted to know just then was whether my love loved me—whether she ever could—whether such happiness was possible under heaven!

"You remember all that mystery about the cargo?" she continued eagerly, her pretty lips so divinely parted!

"It turned out to be gunpowder," said I, still thinking only of her.

"No—gold!"

"But it *was* gunpowder," I insisted; for it was my incorrigible passion for accuracy which had led up to half our arguments on the voyage; but this time Eva let me off.

"It was also gold: twelve thousand ounces from the diggings. That was the real mystery. Do you mean to say you never guessed?"

"No, by Jove I didn't!" said I. She had diverted my interest at last. I asked her if she had known on board.

"Not until the last moment. I found out during the fire. Do you remember when we said good-by? I was nearly telling you then."

Did I remember! The very letter of that last interview was cut deep in my heart; not a sleep-

In the Garden

less night had I passed without rehearsing it word
for word and look for look; and sometimes, when
sorrow had spent itself, and the heart could bleed
no more, vain grief had given place to vainer
speculation, and I had cudgelled my wakeful
brains for the meaning of the new and subtle
horror which I had read in my darling's eyes at
the last. Now I understood; and the one explanation brought such a tribe in its train, that even the
perilous ecstasy of the present moment was temporarily forgotten in the horrible past.

"Now I know why they wouldn't have me in
the gig!" I cried softly.

"She carried four heavy men's weight in gold."

"When on earth did they get it aboard?"

"In provision boxes at the last; but they had
been filling the boxes for weeks."

"Why, I saw them doing it!" I cried. "But
what about the gig? Who picked you up?"

She was watching that open door once more,
and she answered with notable indifference, "Mr.
Rattray."

"So that's the connection!" said I; and I think
its very simplicity was what surprised me most.

"Yes; he was waiting for us at Ascension."

"Then it was all arranged?"

"Every detail."

Dead Men Tell No Tales

"And this young blackguard is as bad as any of them!"

"Worse," said she, with bitter brevity. Nor had I ever seen her look so hard but once, and that was the night before in the old justice hall, when she told Rattray her opinion of him to his face. She had now the same angry flush, the same set mouth and scornful voice; and I took it finally into my head that she was unjust to the poor devil, villain though he was. With all his villainy I declined to believe him as bad as the others. I told her so in as many words. And in a moment we were arguing as though we were back on the *Lady Jermyn* with nothing else to do.

"You may admire wholesale murderers and thieves," said Eva. "I do not."

"Nor I. My point is simply that this one is not as bad as the rest. I believe he was really glad for my sake when he discovered that I knew nothing of the villainy. Come now, has he ever offered you any personal violence?"

"Me? Mr. Rattray? I should hope not, indeed!"

"Has he never saved you from any?"

"I—I don't know."

"Then I do. When you left them last night there was some talk of bringing you back by force.

In the Garden

You can guess who suggested that—and who set his face against it and got his way. You would think the better of Rattray had you heard what passed."

"Should I?" she asked half eagerly, as she looked quickly round at me; and suddenly I saw her eyes fill. "Oh, why will you speak about him?" she burst out. "Why must you defend him, unless it's to go against me, as you always did and always will! I never knew anybody like you—never! I want you to take me away from these wretches, and all you do is to defend them!"

"Not all," said I, clasping her hand warmly in mine. "Not all—not all! I will take you away from them, never fear; in another hour God grant you may be out of their reach for ever!"

"But where are we to go?" she whispered wildly. "What are you to do with me? All my friends think me dead, and if they knew I was not it would all come out."

"So it shall," said I; "the sooner the better; if I'd had my way it would all be out already."

I see her yet, my passionate darling, as she turned upon me, whiter than the full white moon.

"Mr. Cole," said she, "you must give me your sacred promise that so far as you are concerned, it shall never come out at all!"

Dead Men Tell No Tales

"This monstrous conspiracy? This cold-blooded massacre?"

And I crouched aghast.

"Yes; it could do no good; and, at any rate, unless you promise I remain where I am."

"In their hands?"

"Decidedly—to warn them in time. Leave them I would, but betray them—never!"

What could I say? What choice had I in the face of an alternative so headstrong and so unreasonable? To rescue Eva from these miscreants I would have let every malefactor in the country go unscathed: yet the condition was a hard one; and, as I hesitated, my love went on her knees to me, there in the moonlight among the rhododendrons.

"Promise—promise—or you will kill me!" she gasped. "They may deserve it richly, but I would rather be torn in little pieces than—than have them—hanged!"

"It is too good for most of them."

"Promise!"

"To hold my tongue about them all?"

"Yes—promise!"

"But, Eva——"

"Promise!"

"When a hundred lives were sacrificed——"

In the Garden

"Promise!"

"I can't," I said. "It's wrong."

"Then good-by!" she cried, starting to her feet.

"No—no—" and I caught her hand.

"Well, then?"

"I—promise."

CHAPTER XV

FIRST BLOOD

SO I bound myself to a guilty secrecy for Eva's sake, to save her from these wretches, or if you will, to win her for myself. Nor did it strike me as very strange, after a moment's reflection, that she should intercede thus earnestly for a band headed by her own mother's widower, prime scoundrel of them all though she knew him to be. The only surprise was that she had not interceded in his name; that I should have forgotten, and she should have allowed me to forget, the very existence of so indisputable a claim upon her loyalty. This, however, made it a little difficult to understand the hysterical gratitude with which my unwilling promise was received. Poor darling! she was beside herself with sheer relief. She wept as I had never seen her weep before. She seized and even kissed my hands, as one who neither knew nor cared what she did, surprising me so much by her emotion that this expression of it passed unheeded. I was the best friend she had ever had. I was her one good friend in all the

First Blood

world; she would trust herself to me; and if I would but take her to the convent where she had been brought up, she would pray for me there until her death, but that would not be very long.

All of which confused me utterly; it seemed an inexplicable breakdown in one who had shown such nerve and courage hitherto, and so hearty a loathing for that damnable Santos. So completely had her presence of mind forsaken her that she looked no longer where she had been gazing hitherto. And thus it was that neither of us saw José until we heard him calling, "Senhora Evah! Senhora Evah!" with some rapid sentences in Portuguese.

"Now is our time," I whispered, crouching lower and clasping a small hand gone suddenly cold. "Think of nothing now but getting out of this. I'll keep my word once we are out; and here's the toy that's going to get us out." And I produced my Deane and Adams with no small relish.

A little trustful pressure was my answer and my reward; meanwhile the black was singing out lustily in evident suspicion and alarm.

"He says they are coming back," whispered Eva; but that's impossible."

"Why?"

Dead Men Tell No Tales

"Because if they were he couldn't see them, and if he heard them he would be frightened of their hearing him. But here he comes!"

A shuffling quick step on the path; a running grumble of unmistakable threats; a shambling moonlit figure seen in glimpses through the leaves, very near us for an instant, then hidden by the shrubbery as he passed within a few yards of our hiding-place. A diminuendo of the shuffling steps; then a cursing, frightened savage at one end of the rhododendrons, and we two stealing out at the other, hand in hand, and bent quite double, into the long neglected grass.

"Can you run for it?" I whispered.

"Yes, but not too fast, for fear we trip."

"Come on, then!"

The lighted open doorway grew greater at every stride.

"He hasn't seen us yet——"

"No, I hear him threatening me still."

"Now he has, though!"

A wild whoop proclaimed the fact, and upright we tore at top speed through the last ten yards of grass, while the black rushed down one of the side paths, gaining audibly on us over the better ground. But our start had saved us, and we flew up the steps as his feet ceased to clatter on the

First Blood

path; he had plunged into the grass to cut off the corner.

"Thank God!" cried Eva. "Now shut it quick."

The great door swung home with a mighty clatter, and Eva seized the key in both hands.

"I can't turn it!"

To lose a second was to take a life, and unconsciously I was sticking at that, perhaps from no higher instinct than distrust of my aim. Our pursuer, however, was on the steps when I clapped my free hand on top of those little white straining ones, and by a timely effort bent both them and the key round together; the ward shot home as José hurled himself against the door. Eva bolted it. But the thud was not repeated, and I gathered myself together between the door and the nearest window, for by now I saw there was but one thing for us. The nigger must be disabled, if I could manage such a nicety; if not, the devil take his own.

Well, I was not one tick too soon for him. My pistol was not cocked before the crash came that I was counting on, and with it a shower of small glass driving across the six-foot sill and tinkling on the flags. Next came a black and bloody face, at which I could not fire. I had to wait till I saw his legs, when I promptly shattered one of them at disgracefully short range. The report was as deafening as one upon the stage; the hall filled with white smoke, and remained hideous with the bellowing of my victim. I searched him without a qualm, but threats of annihilation instead, and found him unarmed but for that very knife which Rattray had induced me to hand over to him in town. I had a grim satisfaction in depriving him of this, and but small compunction in turning my back upon his pain.

"Come," I said to poor Eva, "don't pity him, though I daresay he's the most pitiable of the lot; show me the way through, and I'll follow with this lamp."

One was burning on the old oak table. I carried it along a narrow passage, through a great low kitchen where I bumped my head against the black oak beams; and I held it on high at a door almost as massive as the one which we had succeeded in shutting in the nigger's face.

"I was afraid of it!" cried Eva, with a sudden sob.

"What is it?"

"They've taken away the key!"

Yes, the keen air came through an empty keyhole; and my lamp, held close, not only showed

First Blood

us that the door was locked, but that the lock was one with which an unskilled hand might tamper for hours without result. I dealt it a hearty kick by way of a test. The heavy timber did not budge; there was no play at all at either lock or hinges; nor did I see how I could spend one of my four remaining bullets upon the former, with any chance of a return.

"Is this the only other door?"

"Yes."

"Then it must be a window."

"All the back ones are barred."

"Securely?"

"Yes."

"Then we've no choice in the matter."

And I led the way back to the hall, where the poor black devil lay blubbering in his blood. In the kitchen I found the bottle of wine (Rattray's best port, that they were trying to make her take for her health) with which Eva had bribed him, and I gave it to him before laying hands on a couple of chairs.

"What are you going to do?"

"Go out the way we came."

"But the wall?"

"Pile up these chairs, and as many more as we may need, if we can't open the gate."

Dead Men Tell No Tales

But Eva was not paying attention any longer, either to me or to José; his white teeth were showing in a grin for all his pain; her eyes were fixed in horror on the floor.

"They've come back," she gasped. "The underground passage! Hark—hark!"

There was a muffled rush of feet beneath our own, then a dull but very distinguishable clatter on some invisible stair.

"Underground passage!" I exclaimed, and in my sheer disgust I forgot what was due to my darling. "Why on earth didn't you tell me of it before?"

"There was so much to tell you! It leads to the sea. Oh, what shall we do? You must hide—upstairs—anywhere!" cried Eva, wildly. "Leave them to me—leave them to me."

"I like that," said I; and I did; but I detested myself for the tears my words had drawn, and I prepared to die for them.

"They'll kill you, Mr. Cole!"

"It would serve me right; but we'll see about it."

And I stood with my revolver very ready in my right hand, while with the other I caught poor Eva to my side, even as a door flew open, and Rattray himself burst upon us, a lantern in his hand, and the perspiration shining on his handsome face in its light.

I can see him now as he stood dumfounded on the threshold of the hall; and yet, at the time, my eyes sped past him into the room beyond.

It was the one I have described as being lined with books; there was a long rent in this lining, where the books had opened with a door, through which Captain Harris, Joaquin Santos, and Jane Braithwaite followed Rattray in quick succession, the men all with lanterns, the woman scarlet and dishevelled even for her. It was over the squire's shoulders I saw their faces; he kept them from passing him in the doorway by a free use of his elbows; and when I looked at him again, his black eyes were blazing from a face white with passion, and they were fixed upon me.

"What the devil brings you here?" he thundered at last.

"Don't ask idle questions," was my reply to that.

"So you were shamming to-day!"

"I was taking a leaf out of your book."

"You'll gain nothing by being clever!" sneered the squire, taking a threatening step forward. For at the last moment I had tucked my revolver behind my back, not only for the pleasure, but for the obvious advantage of getting them all in

front of me and off their guard. I had no idea
that such eyes as Rattray's could be so fierce: they
were dancing from me to my companion, whom
their glitter frightened into an attempt to disen-
gage herself from me; but my arm only tightened
about her drooping figure.

"I shall gain no more than I expect," said I,
carelessly. "And I know what to expect from
brave gentlemen like you! It will be better than
your own fate, at all events; anything's better than
being taken hence to the place of execution, and
hanged by the neck until you're dead, all three of
you in a row, and your bodies buried within the
precincts of the prison!"

"The very thing for him," murmured Santos.
"The—very—theeng!"

"But I'm so soft-hearted," I went insanely on,
"that I should be sorry to see that happen to such
fine fellows as you are. Come out of that, you
little fraud behind there!" It was my betrayer
skulking in the room. "Come out and line up
with the rest! No, I'm not going to see you fellows dance on nothing; I've another kind of ball
apiece for you, and one between 'em for the
Braithwaites!"

Well, I suppose I always had a nasty tongue
me, and rather enjoyed making play with it

on provocation; but, if so, I met with my deserts that night. For the nigger of the *Lady Jermyn* lay all but hid behind Eva and me; if they saw him at all, they may have thought him drunk; but, as for myself, I had fairly forgotten his existence until the very moment came for showing my revolver, when it was twisted out of my grasp instead, and a ball sang under my arm as the brute fell back exhausted and the weapon clattered beside him. Before I could stoop for it there was a dead weight on my left arm, and Squire Rattray was over the table at a bound, with his arms jostling mine beneath Eva Denison's senseless form.

"Leave her to me," he cried fiercely. "You fool," he added in a lower key, "do you think I'd let any harm come to her?"

I looked him in the bright and honest eyes that had made me trust him in the beginning. And I did not utterly distrust him yet. Rather was the guile on my side as I drew back and watched Rattray lift the young girl tenderly, and slowly carry her to the door by which she had entered and left the hall just twenty-four hours before. I could not take my eyes off them till they were gone. And when I looked for my revolver, it also had disappeared.

Dead Men Tell No Tales

José had not got it—he lay insensible. Santos was whispering to Harris. Neither of them seemed armed. I made sure that Rattray had picked it up and carried it off with Eva. I looked wildly for some other weapon. Two unarmed men and a woman were all I had to deal with, for Braithwaite had long since vanished. Could I but knock the worthless life out of the men, I should have but the squire and his servants to deal with; and in that quarter I still had my hopes of a bloodless battle and a treaty of war.

A log fire was smouldering in the open grate. I darted to it, and had a heavy, half-burned brand whirling round my head next instant. Harris was the first within my reach. He came gamely at me with his fists. I sprang upon him, and struck him to the ground with one blow, the sparks flying far and wide as my smoking brand met the seaman's skull. Santos was upon me next instant, and him, by sheer luck, I managed to serve the same; but I doubt whether either man was stunned; and I was standing ready for them to rise, when I felt myself seized round the neck from behind, and a mass of fluffy hair tickling my cheek, while a shrill voice set up a lusty scream for the squire.

I have said that the woman Braithwaite was

First Blood

of a sinister strength; but I had little dreamt how strong she really was. First it was her arms that wound themselves about my neck, long, sinuous, and supple as the tentacles of some vile monster; then, as I struggled, her thumbs were on my windpipe like pads of steel. Tighter she pressed, and tighter yet. My eyeballs started; my tongue lolled; I heard my brand drop, and through a mist I saw it picked up instantly. It crashed upon my skull as I still struggled vainly; again and again it came down mercilessly in the same place; until I felt as though a sponge of warm water had been squeezed over my head, and saw a hundred withered masks grinning sudden exultation into mine; but still the lean arm whirled, and the splinters flew, till I was blind with my blood and the seven senses were beaten out of me.

CHAPTER XVI

A DEADLOCK

IT must have been midnight when I opened
my eyes; a clock was striking as though it
never would stop. My mouth seemed fire; a pun-
gent flavor filled my nostrils; the wineglass felt
cold against my teeth. "That's more like it!"
muttered a voice close to my ear. An arm was
withdrawn from under my shoulders. I was allowed to sink back upon some pillows. And now
I saw where I was. The room was large and
poorly lighted. I lay in my clothes on an old
four-poster bed. And my enemies were standing
over me in a group.

"I hope you are satisfied!" sneered Joaquin
Santos, with a flourish of his eternal cigarette.

"I am. You don't do murder in my house,
wherever else you may do it."

"And now better lid 'im to the nirrest poliss-
station; or weel you go and tell the poliss yourself?" asked the Portuguese, in the same tone of
mordant irony.

A Deadlock

"Ay, ay," growled Harris; "that's the next thing!"

"No," said Rattray; "the next thing's for you two to leave him to me."

"We'll see you damned!" cried the captain.

"No, no, my friend," said Santos, with a shrug; "let him have his way. He is as fond of his skeen as you are of yours; he'll come round to our way in the end. I know this Senhor Cole. It is necessary for 'im to die. But it is not necessary this moment; let us live them together for a leetle beet."

"That's all I ask," said Rattray.

"You won't ask it twice," rejoined Santos, shrugging. "I know this Senhor Cole. There is only one way of dilling with a man like that. Besides, he 'as 'alf-keeled my good José; it is necessary for 'im to die."

"I agree with the senhor," said Harris, whose forehead was starred with sticking-plaster. "It's him or us, an' we're all agen you, squire. You'll have to give in, first or last."

And the pair were gone; their steps grew faint in the corridor; when we could no longer hear them, Rattray closed the door and quietly locked it. Then he turned to me, stern enough, and pointed to the door with a hand that shook.

Dead Men Tell No Tales

"You see how it is?"

"Perfectly."

"They want to kill you!"

"Of course they do."

"It's your own fault; you've run yourself into this. I did my best to keep you out of it. But in you come, and spill first blood."

"I don't regret it," said I.

"Oh, you're damned mule enough not to regret anything!" cried Rattray. "I see the sort you are; yet but for me, I tell you plainly, you'd be a dead man now."

"I can't think why you interfered."

"You've heard the reason. I won't have murder done here if I can prevent it; so far I have; it rests with you whether I can go on preventing it or not."

"With me, does it?"

He sat down on the side of the bed. He threw an arm to the far side of my body, and he leaned over me with savage eyes now staring into mine, now resting with a momentary gleam of pride upon my battered head. I put up my hand; it lit upon a very turban of bandages, and at that I tried to take his hand in mine. He shook it off, and his eyes met mine more fiercely than before.

"See here, Cole," said he; "I don't know how

A Deadlock

the devil you got wind of anything to start with, and I don't care. What I do know is that you've made bad enough a long chalk worse for all concerned, and you'll have to get yourself out of the mess you've got yourself into, and there's only one way. I suppose Miss Denison has really told you everything this time? What's that? Oh, yes, she's all right again; no thanks to you. Now let's hear what she did tell you. It'll save time."

I repeated the hurried disclosures made by Eva in the rhododendrons. He nodded grimly in confirmation of their truth.

"Yes, those are the rough facts. The game was started in Melbourne. My part was to wait at Ascension till the *Lady Jermyn* signalled herself, follow her in a schooner we had bought and pick up the gig with the gold aboard. Well, I did so; never mind the details now, and never mind the bloody massacre the others had made of it before I came up. God knows I was never a consenting party to that, though *I* know I'm responsible. I'm in this thing as deep as any of them. I've shared the risks and I'm going to share the plunder, and I'll swing with the others if it ever comes to that. I deserve it hard enough. And so here we are, we three and the nigger, all four fit to swing in a row, as you were fool enough to tell us; and

you step in and find out everything. What's to
be done? You know what the others want to do.
I say it rests with you whether they do it or not.
There's only one other way of meeting the case."

"What's that?"

"Be in it yourself, man! Come in with me and
split my share!"

I could have burst out laughing in his handsome, eager face; the good faith of this absurd
proposal was so incongruously apparent; and so
obviously genuine was the young villain's anxiety
for my consent. Become accessory after the fact
in such a crime! Sell my silence for a price! I
concealed my feelings with equal difficulty and
resolution. I had plans of my own already, but
I must gain time to think them over. Nor could
I afford to quarrel with Rattray meanwhile.

"What was the haul?" I asked him, with the
air of one not unprepared to consider the matter.

"Twelve thousand ounces!"

"Forty-eight thousand pounds, about?"

"Yes—yes."

"And your share?"

"Fourteen thousand pounds. Santos takes
twenty, and Harris and I fourteen thousand each."

"And you offer me seven?"

"I do! I do!"

A Deadlock

He was becoming more and more eager and excited. His eyes were brighter than I had ever seen them, but slightly bloodshot, and a coppery flush tinged his clear, sunburnt skin. I fancied he had been making somewhat free with the brandy. But loss of blood had cooled my brain; and, perhaps, natural perversity had also a share in the composure which grew upon me as it deserted my companion.

"Why make such a sacrifice?" said I, smiling. "Why not let them do as they like?"

"I've told you why! I'm not so bad as all that. I draw the line at bloody murder! Not a life should have been lost if I'd had my way. Besides, I've done all the dirty work by you, Cole; there's been no help for it. We didn't know whether you knew or not; it made all the difference to us; and somebody had to dog you and find out how much you did know. I was the only one who could possibly do it. God knows how I detested the job! I'm more ashamed of it than of worse things. I had to worm myself into your friendship; and, by Jove, you made me think you *did* know, but hadn't let it out, and might any day. So then I got you up here, where you would be in our power if it was so; surely you can see every move? But this much I'll swear—I had nothing to do with José breaking into your room at the hotel; they went behind me there, curse them! And when at last I found out for certain, down here, that you knew nothing after all, I was never more sincerely thankful in my life. I give you my word it took a load off my heart."

"I know that," I said. "I also know who broke into my room, and I'm glad I'm even with one of you."

"It's done you no good," said Rattray. "Their first thought was to put you out of the way, and it's more than ever their last. You see the sort of men you've got to deal with; and they're three to one, counting the nigger; but if you go in with me they'll only be three to two."

He was manifestly anxious to save me in this fashion. And I suppose that most sensible men, in my dilemma, would at least have nursed or played upon good-will so lucky and so enduring. But there was always a twist in me that made me love (in my youth) to take the unexpected course; and it amused me the more to lead my young friend on.

"And where have you got this gold?" I asked him, in a low voice so promising that he instantly lowered his, and his eyes twinkled naughtily into mine.

A Deadlock

"In the old tunnel that runs from this place nearly to the sea," said he. "We Rattrays have always been a pretty warm lot, Cole, and in the old days we were the most festive smugglers on the coast; this tunnel's a relic of 'em, although it was only a tradition till I came into the property. I swore I'd find it, and when I'd done so I made the new connection which you shall see. I'm rather proud of it. And I won't say I haven't used the old drain once or twice after the fashion of my rude forefathers; but never was it such a godsend as it's been this time. By Jove, it would be a sin if you didn't come in with us, Cole; but for the lives these blackguards lost the thing's gone splendidly; it would be a sin if you went and lost yours, whereas, if you come in, the two of us would be able to shake off those devils: we should be too strong for 'em."

"Seven thousand pounds!" I murmured. "Forty-eight thousand between us!"

"Yes, and nearly all of it down below, at this end of the tunnel, and the rest where we dropped it when we heard you were trying to bolt. We'd got it all at the other end, ready to pop aboard the schooner that's lying there still, if you turned out to know anything and to have told what you knew to the police. There was always the possibility of that, you see; we simply daren't show our noses at the bank until we knew how much *you* knew, and what you'd done or were thinking of doing. As it is, we can take 'em the whole twelve thousand ounces, or rather I can, as soon as I like, in broad daylight. I'm a lucky digger. It's all right. Everybody knows I've been out there. They'll have to pay me over the counter; and if you wait in the cab, by the Lord Harry, I'll pay you your seven thousand first! You don't deserve it, Cole, but you shall have it, and between us we'll see the others to blazes!"

He jumped up all excitement, and was at the door next instant.

"Stop!" I cried. "Where are you going?"

"Downstairs to tell them."

"Tell them what?"

"That you're going in with me, and it's all right."

"And do you really think I am?"

He had unlocked the door; after a pause I heard him lock it again. But I did not see his face until he returned to the bedside. And then it frightened me. It was distorted and discolored with rage and chagrin.

"You've been making a fool of me!" he cried fiercely.

A Deadlock

"No, I have been considering the matter, Rattray."

"And you won't accept my offer?"

"Of course I won't. I didn't say I'd been considering that."

He stood over me with clenched fists and starting eyes.

"Don't you see that I want to save your life?" he cried. "Don't you see that this is the only way? Do you suppose a murder more or less makes any difference to that lot downstairs? Are you really such a fool as to die rather than hold your tongue?"

"I won't hold it for money, at all events," said I. "But that's what I was coming to."

"Very well!" he interrupted. "You shall only pretend to touch it. All I want is to convince the others that it's against your interest to split. Self-interest is the one motive they understand. Your bare word would be good enough for me."

"Suppose I won't give my bare word?" said I, in a gentle manner which I did not mean to be as irritating as it doubtless was. Yet his proposals and his assumptions were between them making me irritable in my turn.

"For Heaven's sake don't be such an idiot, Cole!" he burst out in a passion. "You know I'm against the others, and you know what they want, yet you do your best to put me on their side! You know what they are, and yet you hesitate! For the love of God be sensible; as least give me your word that you'll hold your tongue for ever about all you know."

"All right," I said. "I'll give you my word— my sacred promise, Rattray—on one condition."

"What's that?"

"That you let me take Miss Denison away from you, for good and all!"

His face was transformed with fury: honest passion faded from it and left it bloodless, deadly, sinister.

"Away from me?" said Rattray, through his teeth.

"From the lot of you."

"I remember! You told me that night. Ha, ha, ha! You were in love with her—you—you!"

"That has nothing to do with it," said I, shaking the bed with my anger and my agitation.

"I should hope not! *You,* indeed, to look at *her!*"

"Well," I cried, "she may never love me; but at least she doesn't loathe me as she loathes you —yes, and the sight of you, and your very name!"

So I drew blood for blood; and for an instant

A Deadlock

I thought he was going to make an end of it by incontinently killing me himself. His fists flew out. Had I been a whole man on my legs, he took care to tell me what he would have done, and to drive it home with a mouthful of the oaths which were conspicuously absent from his ordinary talk.

"You take advantage of your weakness, like any cur," he wound up.

"And you of your strength—like the young bully you are!" I retorted.

"You do your best to make me one," he answered bitterly. "I try to stand by you at all costs. I want to make amends to you, I want to prevent a crime. Yet there you lie and set your face against a compromise; and there you lie and taunt me with the thing that's gall and wormwood to me already. I know I gave you provocation. And I know I'm rightly served. Why do you suppose I went into this accursed thing at all? Not for the gold, my boy, but for the girl! So she won't look at me. And it serves me right. But—I say—do you really think she *loathes* me, Cole?"

"I don't see how she can think much better of you than of the crime in which you've had a hand," was my reply, made, however, with much kindness as I could summon. "The word

Dead Men Tell No Tales

I used was spoken in anger," said I; for his had
disappeared; and he looked such a miserable,
handsome dog as he stood there hanging his
guilty head—in the room, I fancied, where he
once had lain as a pretty, innocent child.

"Cole," said he, "I'd give twice my share of
the damned stuff never to have put my hand to
the plough; but go back I can't; so there's an end
of it."

"I don't see it," said I. "You say you didn't
go in for the gold? Then give up your share;
the others'll jump at it; and Eva won't think the
worse of you, at any rate."

"But what's to become of her if I drop
out?"

"You and I will take her to her friends, or
wherever she wants to go."

"No, no!" he cried. "I never yet deserted my
pals, and I'm not going to begin."

"I don't believe you ever before had such pals
to desert," was my reply to that. "Quite apart
from my own share in the matter, it makes me
positively sick to see a fellow like you mixed up
with such a crew in such a game. Get out of it,
man, get out of it while you can! Now's your
time. Get out of it, for God's sake!"

I sat up in my eagerness. I saw him waver.

A Deadlock

And for one instant a great hope fluttered in my heart. But his teeth met. His face darkened. He shook his head.

"That's the kind of rot that isn't worth talking, and you ought to know it," said he. "When I begin a thing I go through with it, though it lands me in hell, as this one will. I can't help that. It's too late to go back. I'm going on; and you're going with me, Cole, like a sensible chap!"

I shook my head.

"Only on the one condition."

"You-stick-to-that?" he said, so rapidly that the words ran into one, so fiercely that his decision was as plain to me as my own.

"I do," said I, and could only sigh when he made yet one more effort to persuade me, in a distress not less apparent than his resolution, and not less becoming in him.

"Consider, Cole, consider!"

"I have already done so, Rattray."

"Murder is simply nothing to them!"

"It is nothing to me either."

"Human life is nothing!"

"No; it must end one day."

"You won't give your word unconditionally?"

"No; you know my condition."

Dead Men Tell No Tales

He ignored it with a blazing eye, his hand upon the door.

"You prefer to die, then?"

"Infinitely."

"Then die you may, and be damned to you!"

CHAPTER XVII

WHEN THIEVES FALL OUT

THE door slammed. It was invisibly locked, and the key taken out. I listened for the last of an angry stride. It never even began. But after a pause the door was unlocked again, and Rattray re-entered.

Without looking at me, he snatched the candle from the table on which it stood by the bedside, and carried it to a bureau at the opposite side of the room. There he stood a minute with his back turned, the candle, I fancy, on the floor. I saw him putting something in either jacket pocket. Then I heard a dull little snap, as though he had shut some small morocco case; whatever it was, he tossed it carelessly back into the bureau; and next minute he was really gone, leaving the candle burning on the floor.

I lay and heard his steps out of earshot, and they were angry enough now, nor had he given me a single glance. I listened until there was no more to be heard, and then in an instant I was off the bed and on my feet. I reeled a little, and my head gave me great pain, but greater still was my excitement. I caught up the candle, opened the unlocked bureau, and then the empty case which I found in the very front.

My heart leapt; there was no mistaking the depressions in the case. It was a brace of tiny pistols that Rattray had slipped into his jacket pockets.

Mere toys they must have been in comparison with my dear Deane and Adams; that mattered nothing. I went no longer in dire terror of my life; indeed, there was that in Rattray which had left me feeling fairly safe, in spite of his last words to me, albeit I felt his fears on my behalf to be genuine enough. His taking these little pistols (of course, there were but three chambers left loaded in mine) confirmed my confidence in him.

He would stick at nothing to defend me from the violence of his bloodthirsty accomplices. But it should not come to that. My legs were growing firmer under me. I was not going to lie there meekly without making at least an effort at self-deliverance. If it succeeded—the idea came to me in a flash—I would send Rattray an ultimatum from the nearest town; and either Eva should be set instantly and unconditionally free, or the whole matter be put unreservedly in the hands of the local police.

There were two lattice windows, both in the same immensely thick wall; to my joy, I discovered that they overlooked the open premises at the back of the hall, with the oak-plantation beyond; nor was the distance to the ground very great. It was the work of a moment to tear the sheets from the bed, to tie the two ends together and a third round the mullion by which the larger window was bisected. I had done this, and had let down my sheets, when a movement below turned my heart to ice. The night had clouded over. I could see nobody; so much the greater was my alarm.

I withdrew from the window, leaving the sheets hanging, in the hope that they also might be invisible in the darkness. I put out the candle, and returned to the window in great perplexity. Next moment I stood agh ——between the devil and the deep sea. I still heard a something down below, but a worse sound came to drown it. An unseen hand was very quietly trying the door which Rattray had locked behind him.

"Diablo!" came to my horrified ears, in a soft, vindictive voice.

Dead Men Tell No Tales

"I told ye so," muttered another; "the young swab's got the key."

There was a pause, in which it would seem that Joaquin Santos had his ear at the empty keyhole.

"I think he must be slipping," at last I heard him sigh. "It was not necessary to awaken him in this world. It is a peety."

"One kick over the lock would do it," said Harris; "only the young swab'll hear."

"Not perhaps while he is dancing attendance on the senhora. Was it not good to send him to her? If he does hear, well, his own turn will come the queecker, that is all. But it would be better to take them one at a time; so keeck away, my friend, and I will give him no time to squil."

While my would-be murderers were holding this whispered colloquy, I had stood half-petrified by the open window; unwilling to slide down the sheets into the arms of an unseen enemy, though I had no idea which of them it could be; more hopeful of slipping past my butchers in the darkness, and so to Rattray and poor Eva; but not the less eagerly looking for some hiding-place in the room. The best that offered was a recess in the thick wall between the two windows, filled with hanging clothes: a narrow closet without a door,

202

which would shelter me well enough if not too curiously inspected. Here I hid myself in the end, after a moment of indecision which nearly cost me my life. The coats and trousers still shook in front of me when the door flew open at the first kick, and Santos stood a moment in the moonlight, looking for the bed. With a stride he reached it, and I saw the gleam of a knife from where I stood among the squire's clothes; it flashed over my bed, and was still.

"He is not 'ere!"

"He heard us, and he's a-hiding."

"Make light, my friend, and we shall very soon see."

Harris did so.

"Here's a candle," said Santos; "light it, and watch the door. Perro mal dicto! What have we here?"

I felt certain he had seen me, but the candle passed within a yard of my feet, and was held on high at the open window.

"We are too late!" said Santos. "He's gone!"

"Are you sure?"

"Look at this sheet."

"Then the other swab knew of it, and we'll settle with him."

"Yes, yes. But not yet, my good friend—not

yet. We want his asseestance in getting the gold back to the sea; he will be glad enough to give it, now that his pet bird has flown; after that—by all mins. You shall cut his troth, and I will put one of 'is dear friend's bullets in 'im for my own satisfaction."

There was a quick step on the stairs—in the corridor.

"I'd like to do it now," whispered Harris; "no time like the present."

"Not yet, I tell you!"

And Rattray was in the room, a silver-mounted pistol in each hand; the sight of these was a surprise to his treacherous confederates, as even I could see.

"What the devil are you two doing here?" he thundered.

"We thought he was too quite," said Santos. "You percive the rizzon."

And he waved from empty bed to open window, then held the candle close to the tied sheet, and shrugged expressively.

"You thought he was too quiet!" echoed Rattray with fierce scorn. "You thought I was too blind—that's what you mean. To tell me that Miss Denison wished to see me, and Miss Denison that I wished to speak to her! As if we

When Thieves Fall Out

shouldn't find you out in about a minute! But a
minute was better than nothing, eh? And you've
made good use of your minute, have you. You've
murdered him, and you pretend he's got out? By
God, if you have, I'll murder you! I've been
ready for this all night!"

And he stood with his back to the window, his
pistols raised, and his head carried proudly—happily—like a man whose self-respect was coming
back to him after many days. Harris shrank before his fierce eyes and pointed barrels. The
Portuguese, however, had merely given a characteristic shrug, and was now rolling the inevitable cigarette.

"Your common sense is almost as remarkable
as your sense of justice, my friend," said he.
"You see us one, two, tree meenutes ago, and you
see us now. You see the empty bed, the empty
room, and you imagine that in one, two, tree
meenutes we have killed a man and disposed of
his body. Truly, you are very wise and just, and
very loyal also to your friends. You treat a
dangerous enemy as though he were your tween-
brother. You let him escape—let him, I repit—
and then you threaten to shoot those who, as it is,
may pay for your carelessness with their lives.
We have been always very loyal to you, Senhor

Dead Men Tell No Tales

Rattray. We have leestened to your advice, and often taken it against our better judgment. We are here, not because we think it wise, but because you weeshed it. Yet at the first temptation you turn upon us, you point your peestols at your friends."

"I don't believe in your loyalty," rejoined Rattray. "I believe you would shoot me sooner than I would you. The only difference would be that I should be shot in the back!"

"It is untrue," said Santos, with immense emotion. "I call the saints to witness that never by thought or word have I been disloyal to you"— and the blasphemous wretch actually crossed himself with a trembling, skinny hand. "I have leestened to you, though you are the younger man. I have geeven way to you in everything from the moment we were so fullish as to set foot on this accursed coast; that also was your doeeng; and it will be your fault if ivil comes of it. Yet I have not complained. Here in your own 'ouse you have been the master, I the guest. So far from plotting against you, show me the man who has heard me brith one treacherous word behind your back; you will find it deeficult, friend Rattray; what do you say, captain?"

"Me?" cried Harris, in a voice bursting with

abuse. And what the captain said may or may not be imagined. It cannot be set down.

But the man who ought to have spoken—the man who had such a chance as few men have off the stage—who could have confounded these villains in a breath, and saved the wretched Rattray at once from them and from himself—that unheroic hero remained ignobly silent in his homely hiding-place. And, what is more, he would do the same again!

The rogues had fallen out; now was the time for honest men. They all thought I had escaped; therefore they would give me a better chance than ever of still escaping; and I have already explained to what purpose I meant to use my first hours of liberty. That purpose I hold to have justified any ingratitude that I may seem now to have displayed towards the man who had undoubtedly stood between death and me. Was not Eva Denison of more value than many Rattrays? And it was precisely in relation with this pure young girl that I most mistrusted the squire: obviously then my first duty was to save Eva from Rattray, not Rattray from these traitors.

Not that I pretend for a moment to have been the thing I never was: you are not so very grateful to the man who pulls you out of the mud when

Dead Men Tell No Tales

he has first of all pushed you in; nor is it chivalry alone which spurs one to the rescue of a lovely lady for whom, after all, one would rather live than die. Thus I, in my corner, was thinking (I will say) of Eva first; but next I was thinking of myself; and Rattray's blood be on his own hot head! I hold, moreover, that I was perfectly right in all this; but if any think me very wrong, a sufficient satisfaction is in store for them, for I was very swiftly punished.

The captain's language was no worse in character than in effect: the bed was bloody from my wounded head, all tumbled from the haste with which I had quitted it, and only too suggestive of still fouler play. Rattray stopped the captain with a sudden flourish of one of his pistols, the silver mountings making lightning in the room; then he called upon the pair of them to show him what they had done with me; and to my horror, Santos invited him to search the room. The invitation was accepted. Yet there I stood. It would have been better to step forward even then. Yet I cowered among his clothes until his own hand fell upon my collar, and forth I was dragged to the plain amazement of all three.

Santos was the first to find his voice.

When Thieves Fall Out

"Another time you will perhaps think twice before you spik, friend squire."

Rattray simply asked me what I had been doing in there, in a white flame of passion, and with such an oath that I embellished the truth for him in my turn.

"Trying to give you blackguards the slip," said I.

"Then it was you who let down the sheet?"

"Of course it was."

"All right! I'm done with you," said he; "that settles it. I make you an offer. You won't accept it. I do my best; you do your worst; but I'll be shot if you get another chance from me!"

Brandy and the wine-glass stood where Rattray must have set them, on an oak stool beside the bed; as he spoke he crossed the room, filled the glass till the spirit dripped, and drained it at a gulp. He was twitching and wincing still when he turned, walked up to Joaquin Santos, and pointed to where I stood with a fist that shook.

"You wanted to deal with him," said Rattray; "you're at liberty to do so. I'm only sorry I stood in your way."

But no answer, and for once no rings of smoke came from those shrivelled lips: the man had

Dead Men Tell No Tales

rolled and lighted a cigarette since Rattray entered, but it was burning unheeded between his skinny fingers. *I* had his attention, all to myself. He knew the tale that I was going to tell. He was waiting for it; he was ready for me. The attentive droop of his head; the crafty glitter in his intelligent eyes; the depth and breadth of the creased forehead; the knowledge of his resource, the consciousness of my error, all distracted and confounded me so that my speech halted and my voice ran thin. I told Rattray every syllable that these traitors had been saying behind his back, but I told it all very ill; what was worse, and made me worse, I was only too well aware of my own failure to carry conviction with my words.

"And why couldn't you come out and say so?" asked Rattray, as even I knew that he must. "Why wait till now?"

"Ah, why!" echoed Santos, with a smile and a shake of the head; a suspicious tolerance, an ostentatious truce, upon his parchment face. And already he was sufficiently relieved to suck his cigarette alight again.

"You know why," I said, trusting to bluff honesty with the one of them who was not rotten to the core: "because I still meant escaping."

"And then what?" asked Rattray fiercely.

When Thieves Fall Out

"You had given me my chance," I said; "I should have given you yours."

"You would, would you? Very kind of you, Mr. Cole!"

"No, no," said Santos; "not kind, but clever! Clever, spicious, and queeck-weeted beyond belif! Senhor Rattray, we have all been in the dark; we thought we had fool to dil with, but what admirable knave the young man would make! Such readiness, such resource, with his tongue or with his peestol; how useful would it be to us! I am glad you have decided to live him to me, friend Rattray, for I am quite come round to your way of thinking. It is no longer necessary for him to die!"

"You mean that?" cried Rattray keenly.

"Of course I min it. You were quite right. He must join us. But he will when I talk to him.

I could not speak. I was fascinated by this wretch: it was reptile and rabbit with us. Treachery I knew he meant; my death, for one; my death was certain; and yet I could not speak.

"Then talk to him, for God's sake," cried Rattray, "and I shall be only too glad if you can talk some sense into him. I've tried, and failed."

"I shall not fail," said Santos softly. "But it is better that he has a leetle time to think over it

Dead Men Tell No Tales

calmly; better steel for 'im to slip upon it, as you say. Let us live 'im for the night, what there is of it; time enough in the morning."

I could hardly believe my ears; still I knew that it was treachery, all treachery; and the morning I should never see.

"But we can't leave him up here," said Rattray; "it would mean one of us watching him all night."

"Quite so," said Santos. "I will tell you where we could live him, however, if you will allow me to wheesper one leetle moment."

They drew aside; and, as I live, I thought that little moment was to be Rattray's last on earth. I watched, but nothing happened; on the contrary, both men seemed agreed, the Portuguese gesticulating, the Englishman nodding, as they stood conversing at the window. Their faces were strangely reassuring. I began to reason with myself, to rid my mind of mere presentiment and superstition. If these two really were at one about me (I argued) there might be no treachery after all. When I came to think of it, Rattray had been closeted long enough with me to awake the worst suspicions in the breasts of his companions; now that these were allayed, there might be no more bloodshed after all (if, for example,

212

When Thieves Fall Out

I pretended to give in), even though Santos had not cared whose blood was shed a few minutes since. That was evidently the character of the wretch: to compass his ends or to defend his person he would take life with no more compunction than the ordinary criminal takes money; but (and hence) murder for murder's sake was no amusement to him.

My confidence was further restored by Captain Harris; ever a gross ruffian, with no refinements to his rascality, he had been at the brandy bottle after Rattray's example; and now was dozing on the latter's bed, taking his watch below when he could get it, like the good seaman he had been. I was quite sorry for him when the conversation at the window ceased suddenly, and Rattray roused the captain up.

"Watches aft!" said he. "We want that mattress; you can bring it along, while I lead the way with the pillows and things. Come on, Cole!"

"Where to?" I asked, standing firm.

"Where there's no window for you to jump out of, old boy, and no clothes of mine for you to hide behind. You needn't look so scared; it's as dry as a bone, as cellars go. And it's past three o'clock. And you've just got to come."

CHAPTER XVIII

A MAN OF MANY MURDERS

IT was a good-sized wine-cellar, with very little wine in it; only one full bin could I discover. The bins themselves lined but two of the walls, and most of them were covered in with cobwebs, close-drawn like mosquito-curtains. The ceiling was all too low: torpid spiders hung in disreputable parlors, dead to the eye, but loathsomely alive at an involuntary touch. Rats scuttled when we entered, and I had not been long alone when they returned to bear me company. I am not a natural historian, and had rather face a lion with the right rifle than a rat with a stick. My jailers, however, had been kind enough to leave me a lantern, which, set upon the ground (like my mattress), would afford a warning, if not a protection, against the worst; unless I slept; and as yet I had not lain down.

The rascals had been considerate enough, more especially Santos, who had a new manner for me with his revised opinion of my character; it was a manner almost as courtly as that which had em-

A Man of Many Murders

bellished his relations with Eva Denison, and won him my early regard at sea. Moreover, it was at the suggestion of Santos that they had detained me in the hall, for much-needed meat and drink, on the way down. Thereafter they had conducted me through the book-lined door of my undoing, down stone stairs leading to three cellar doors, one of which they had double-locked upon me.

As soon as I durst I was busy with this door; but to no purpose; it was a slab of solid oak, hung on hinges as massive as its lock. It galled me to think that but two doors stood between me and the secret tunnel to the sea: for one of the other two must lead to it. The first, however, was all beyond me, and I very soon gave it up. There was also a very small grating which let in a very little fresh air: the massive foundations had been tunnelled in one place; a rude alcove was the result, with this grating at the end and top of it, some seven feet above the earth floor. Even had I been able to wrench away the bars, it would have availed me nothing, since the aperture formed the segment of a circle whose chord was but a very few inches long. I had nevertheless a fancy for seeing the stars once more and feeling the breath of heaven upon my bandaged temples, which impelled me to search for that which should add a cubit to my stature. And at a glance I descried two packing-cases, rather small and squat, but the pair of them together the very thing for me. To my amazement, however, I could at first move neither one nor the other of these small boxes. Was it that I was weak as water, or that they were heavier than lead? At last I managed to get one of them in my arms—only to drop it with a thud. A side started; a thin sprinkling of yellow dust glittered on the earth. I fetched the lantern: it was gold-dust from Bendigo or from Ballarat.

To me there was horror unspeakable, yet withal a morbid fascination, in the spectacle of the actual booty for which so many lives had been sacrificed before my eyes. Minute followed minute in which I looked at nothing, and could think of nothing, but the stolen bullion at my feet; then I gathered what of the dust I could, pocketed it in pinches to hide my meddlesomeness, and blew the rest away. The box had dropped very much where I had found it; it had exhausted my strength none the less, and I was glad at last to lie down on the mattress, and to wind my body in Rattray's blankets.

I shuddered at the thought of sleep: the rats became so lively the moment I lay still. One ventured so near as to sit up close to the lantern; the light showed its fat white belly, and the thing itself was like a dog begging, as big to my disgusted eyes. And yet, in the midst of these horrors (to me as bad as any that had preceded them), nature overcame me, and for a space my torments ceased.

"He is aslip," a soft voice said.

"Don't wake the poor devil," said another.

"But I weesh to spik with 'im. Senhor Cole! Senhor Cole!"

I opened my eyes. Santos looked of uncanny stature in the low yellow light, from my pillow close to the earth. Harris turned away at my glance; he carried a spade, and began digging near the boxes without more ado, by the light of a second lantern set on one of them: his back was to me from this time on. Santos shrugged a shoulder towards the captain as he opened a campstool, drew up his trousers, and seated himself with much deliberation at the foot of my mattress.

"When you 'ave treasure," said he, "the better thing is to bury it, Senhor Cole. Our young friend upstairs begs to deefer; but he is slipping; it is peety he takes such quantity of brandy! It is leetle wikness of you Engleesh; we in Portugal never touch it, save as a liqueur; therefore we require less slip. Friend squire upstairs is at this moment no better than a porker. Have I made mistake? I thought it was the same word in both languages; but I am glad to see you smile, Senhor Cole; that is good sign. I was going to say, he is so fast aslip up there, that he would not hear us if we were to shoot each other dead!"

And he gave me his paternal smile, benevolent, humorous, reassuring; but I was no longer reassured; nor did I greatly care any more what happened to me. There is a point of last, as well as one of least resistance, and I had reached both points at once.

"Have you shot *him* dead?" I inquired, thinking that if he had, this would precipitate my turn. But he was far from angry; the parchment face crumpled into tolerant smiles; the venerable head shook a playful reproval, as he threw away the cigarette that I am tired of mentioning, and put the last touch to a fresh one with his tongue.

"What question!" said he; "reely, Senhor Cole! But you are quite right: I would have shot him, or cut his troth" (and he shrugged indifference on the point), "if it had not been for you; and yet it would have been your fault! I nid not explain; the poseetion must have explained itself already; besides, it is past. With you two against us—but it is past. You see, I have no longer the excellent

A Man of Many Murders

José. You broke his leg, bad man. I fear it will be necessary to destroy 'im." Santos made a pause; then inquired if he shocked me.

"Not a bit," said I, neither truly nor untruly; "you interest me." And that he did.

"You see," he continued, "I have not the respect of you Engleesh for 'uman life. We will not argue it. I have at least some respect for prejudice. In my youth I had myself such prejudices; but one loses them on the Zambesi. You cannot expect one to set any value upon the life of a black nigger; and when you have keeled a great many Kaffirs, by the lash, with the crocodiles, or what-not, then a white man or two makes less deeference. I acknowledge there were too many on board that sheep; but what was one to do? You have your Engleesh proverb about the dead men and the stories; it was necessary to make clin swip. You see the result."

He shrugged again towards the boxes; but this time, being reminded of them (I supposed), he rose and went over to see how Harris was progressing. The captain had never looked round; neither did he look at Santos. "A leetle dipper," I heard the latter say, "and, perhaps, a few eenches—" but I lost the last epithet. It followed a glance over the shoulder in my direction, and

Dead Men Tell No Tales

immediately preceded the return of Santos to his camp-stool.

"Yes, it is always better to bury treasure," said he once more; but his tone was altered; it was more contemplative; and many smoke-rings came from the shrunk lips before another word; but through them all, his dark eyes, dull with age, were fixed upon me.

"*You* are a treasure!" he exclaimed at last, softly enough, but quickly and emphatically for him, and with a sudden and most diabolical smile.

"So you are going to bury me?"

I had suspected it when first I saw the spade; then not; but since the visit to the hole I had made up my mind to it.

"Bury you? No, not alive," said Santos, in his playfully reproving tone. "It would be necessary to deeg so dip!" he added through his few remaining teeth.

"Well," I said, "you'll swing for it. That's something."

Santos smiled again, benignantly enough this time: in contemplation also: as an artist smiles upon his work. *I* was his!

"You live town," said he; "no one knows where you go. You come down here; no one knows who you are. Your dear friend squire locks you up for the night, but dreenks too much and goes to slip with the key in his pocket; it is there when he wakes; but the preesoner, where is he? He is gone, vanished, escaped in the night, and, like the base fabreec of your own poet's veesion, he lives no trace—is it trace?—be'ind! A leetle earth is so easily bitten down; a leetle more is so easily carried up into the garden; and a beet of nice strong wire might so easily be found in a cellar, and afterwards in the lock! No, Senhor Cole, I do not expect to 'ang. My schims have seldom one seengle flaw. There was just one in the *Lady Jermyn;* there was—Senhor Cole! If there is one this time, and you will be so kind as to point it out, I will—I will run the reesk of shooting you instead of——"

A pinch of his baggy throat, between the fingers and thumbs of both hands, foreshadowed a cleaner end; and yet I could look at him; nay, it was more than I could do *not* to look upon that bloodless face, with the two dry blots upon the parchment, that were never withdrawn from mine.

"No you won't, messmate! If it's him or us for it, let a bullet do it, and let it do it quick, you bloody Spaniard! You can't do the other without me, and my part's done."

Harris was my only hope. I had seen this from

Dead Men Tell No Tales

the first, but my appeal I had been keeping to the very end. And now he was leaving me before a word would come! Santos had gone over to my grave, and there was Harris at the door!

"It is not dip enough," said the Portuguese.

"It's as deep as I mean to make it, with you sittin' there talkin' about it."

And the door stood open.

"Captain!" I screamed. "For Christ's sake, captain!"

He stood there, trembling, yet even now not looking my way.

"Did you ever see a man hanged?" asked Santos, with a vile eye for each of us. "I once hanged fifteen in a row; abominable thifs. And I once poisoned nearly a hundred at one banquet; an untrustworthy tribe; but the hanging was the worse sight and the worse death. Heugh! There was one man—he was no stouter than you are captain——"

But the door slammed; we heard the captain on the stairs; there was a rustle from the leaves outside, and then a silence that I shall not attempt to describe.

And, indeed, I am done with this description: as I live to tell the tale (or spoil it, if I choose) I will make shorter work of this particular business

222

A Man of Many Murders

than I found it at the time. Perverse I may be in old age as in my youth; but on that my agony— my humiliating agony—I decline to dwell. I suffer it afresh as I write. There are the cobwebs on the ceiling, a bloated spider crawling in one: a worse monster is gloating over me: those dull eyes of his, and my own pistol-barrel, cover me in the lamp-light. The crucifix pin is awry in his cravat; that is because he has offered it me to kiss. As a refinement (I feel sure) my revolver is not cocked; and the hammer goes up—up——

He missed me because a lantern was flashed into his eyes through the grating. He wasted the next ball in firing wildly at the light. And the last chamber's load became suddenly too precious for my person; for there were many voices overhead; there were many feet upon the stairs.

Harris came first—head-first—saw me still living as he reeled—hurled himself upon the boxes and one of these into the hole—all far quicker than my pen can write it. The manœuvre, being the captain's, explained itself: on his heels trod Rattray, with one who brought me to my feet like the call of silver trumpets.

"The house is surrounded," says the squire, very quick and quiet; "is this your doing, Cole?"

"I wish it was," said I; "but I can't complain;

223

it's saved my life." And I looked at Santos, standing dignified and alert, my still smoking pistol in his hand.

"Two things to do," says Rattray—"I don't care which." He strode across the cellar and pulled at the one full bin; something slid out, it was a binful of empty bottles, and this time they were allowed to crash upon the floor; the squire stood pointing to a manhole at the back of the bin. "That's one alternative," said he; "but it will mean leaving this much stuff at least," pointing to the boxes, "and probably all the rest at the other end. The other thing's to stop and fight!"

"I fight," said Santos, stalking to the door. "Have you no more ammunition for me, friend Cole? Then I must live you alive; adios, senhor!"

Harris cast a wistful look towards the manhole, not in cowardice, I fancy, but in sudden longing for the sea, the longing of a poor devil of a sailorman doomed to die ashore. I am still sorry to remember that Rattray judged him differently.

"Come on, skipper," said he; "it's all or none aboard the lugger, and I think it will be none. Up you go; wait a second in the room above, and I'll find you an old cutlass. I shan't be longer." He turned to me with a wry smile. "We're not half-armed," he said; "they've caught us fairly on the

A Man of Many Murders

hop; it should be fun! Good-by, Cole; I wish you'd had another round for that revolver. Good-by, Eva!"

And he held out his hand to our love, who had been watching him all this time with eyes of stone; but now she turned her back upon him without a word. His face changed; the stormlight of passion and remorse played upon it for an instant; he made a step towards her, wheeled abruptly, and took me by the shoulder instead.

"Take care of her, Cole," said he. "Whatever happens—take care of her."

I caught him at the foot of the stairs. I do not defend what I did. But I *had* more ammunition; a few wadded bullets, caps, and powder-charges, loose in a jacket pocket; and I thrust them into one of his, upon a sudden impulse, not (as I think) altogether unaccountable, albeit (as I have said) so indefensible.

My back was hardly turned an instant. I had left a statue of unforgiving coldness. I started round to catch in my arms a half-fainting, grief-stricken form, shaken with sobs that it broke my heart to hear. I placed her on the camp-stool. I knelt down and comforted her as well as I could, stroking her hands, my arm about her heaving shoulders, with the gold-brown hair streaming over them. Such hair as it was! So much longer than I had dreamt. So soft—so fine —my soul swam with the sight and touch of it. Well for me that there broke upon us from above such a sudden din as turned my hot blood cold! A wild shout of surprise; an ensuing roar of defiance; shrieks and curses; yells of rage and pain; and pistol-shot after pistol-shot as loud as cannon in the confined space.

I know now that the battle in the hall was a very brief affair; while it lasted I had no sense of time; minutes or moments, they were (God forgive me!) some of the very happiest in all my life. My joy was as profound as it was also selfish and incongruous. The villains were being routed; of that there could be no doubt or question. I hoped Rattray might escape, but for the others no pity stirred in my heart, and even my sneaking sympathy with the squire could take nothing from the joy that was in my heart. Eva Denison was free. I was free. Our oppressors would trouble us no more. We were both lonely; we were both young; we had suffered together and for each other. And here she lay in my arms, her head upon my shoulder, her soft bosom heaving on my own! My blood ran hot and cold by turns. I forgot everything but our freedom and my love.

A Man of Many Murders

I forgot my sufferings, as I would have you all forget them. I am not to be pitied. I have been in heaven on earth. I was there that night, in my great bodily weakness, and in the midst of bloodshed, death, and crime.

"They have stopped!" cried Eva suddenly. "It is over! Oh, if he is dead!"

And she sat upright, with bright eyes starting from a deathly face. I do not think she knew that she had been in my arms at all: any more than I knew that the firing had ceased before she told me. Excited voices were still raised overhead; but some sounded distant, yet more distinct, coming through the grating from the garden; and none were voices that we knew. One poor wretch, on the other hand, we heard plainly groaning to his death; and we looked in each other's eyes with the same thought.

"That's Harris," said I, with, I fear, but little compassion in my tone or in my heart just then.

"Where are the others?" cried Eva piteously.

"God knows," said I; "they may be done for, too."

"If they are!"

"It's better than the death they would have lived to die."

"But only one of them was a wilful murderer!

Dead Men Tell No Tales

Oh, Mr. Cole—Mr. Cole—go and see what has happened; come back and tell me! I dare not come. I will stay here and pray for strength to bear whatever news you may bring me. Go quickly. I will—wait—and pray!"

So I left the poor child on her knees in that vile cellar, white face and straining hands uplifted to the foul ceiling, sweet lips quivering with prayer, eyelids reverently lowered, and the swift tears flowing from beneath them, all in the yellow light of the lantern that stood burning by her side. How different a picture from that which awaited me overhead!

CHAPTER XIX

MY GREAT HOUR

THE library doors were shut, and I closed the secret one behind me before opening the other and peering out through a wrack of bluish smoke; and there lay Captain Harris, sure enough, breathing his last in the arms of one constable, while another was seated on the table with a very wry face, twisting a tourniquet round his arm, from which the blood was dripping like raindrops from the eaves. A third officer stood in the porch, issuing directions to his men without.

"He's over the wall, I tell you! I saw him run up our ladder. After him every man of you —and spread!"

I looked in vain for Rattray and the rest; yet it seemed as if only one of them had escaped. I was still looking when the man in the porch wheeled back into the hall, and instantly caught sight of me at my door.

"Hillo! here's another of them," cried he. "Out you come, young fellow! Your mates are all dead men."

"They're not my mates."

"Never mind; come you out and let's have a look at you."

I did so, and was confronted by a short, thickset man, who recognized me with a smile, but whom I failed to recognize.

"I might have guessed it was Mr. Cole," said he. "I knew you were here somewhere, but I couldn't make head or tail of you through the smoke."

"I'm surprised that you can make head or tail of me at all," said I.

"Then you've quite forgotten the inquisitive parson you met out fishing? You see I found out your name for myself!"

"So it was a detective!"

"It was and is," said the little man, nodding. "Detective or Inspector Royds, if you're any the wiser."

"What has happened? Who has escaped?"

"Your friend Rattray; but he won't get far."

"What of the Portuguese and the nigger?"

I forgot that I had crippled José, but remembered with my words, and wondered the more where he was.

"I'll show you," said Royds. "It was the nigger let us in. We heard him groaning round at

My Great Hour

the back—who smashed his leg? One of our men was at that cellar grating; there was some of them down there; we wanted to find our way down and corner them, but the fat got in the fire too soon. Can you stand something strong? Then come this way."

He led me out into the garden, and to a tangled heap lying in the moonlight, on the edge of the long grass. The slave had fallen on top of his master; one leg lay swathed and twisted; one black hand had but partially relaxed upon the haft of a knife (*the* knife) that stood up hilt-deep in a blacker heart. And in the hand of Santos was still the revolver (my Deane and Adams) which had sent its last ball through the nigger's body.

"They slipped out behind us, all but the one inside," said Royds, ruefully; "I'm hanged if I know yet how it happened—but we were on them next second. Before that the nigger had made us hide him in the grass, but the old devil ran straight into him, and the one fired as the other struck. It's the worst bit of luck in the whole business, and I'm rather disappointed on the whole. I've been nursing the job all this week; had my last look round this very evening, with one of these officers, and only rode back for more to make sure of taking our gentlemen alive. And we've lost three out of four of 'em, and have still to lay hands on the gold! I suppose you didn't know there was any aboard?" he asked abruptly.

"Not before to-night."

"Nor did we till the *Devoren* came in with letters last week, a hundred and thirty days out. She should have been in a month before you, but she got amongst the ice around the Horn. There was a letter of advice about the gold, saying it would probably go in the *Lady Jermyn;* and another about Rattray and his schooner, which had just sailed; the young gentleman was known to the police out there."

"Do you know where the schooner is?"

"Bless you, no, we've had no time to think about her; the man had been seen about town, and we've done well to lay hands on *him* in the time."

"You will do better still when you do lay hands on him," said I, wresting my eyes from the yellow dead face of the foreign scoundrel. The moon shone full upon his high forehead, his shrivelled lips, dank in their death agony, and on the bauble with the sacred device that he wore always in his tie. I recovered my property from the shrunken fingers, and so turned away with a harder heart than I ever had before or since for any creature of Almighty God.

Harris had expired in our absence.

"Never spoke, sir," said the constable in whose arms we had left him.

"More's the pity. Well, cut out at the back and help land the young gent, or we'll have him giving us the slip too. He may double back, but I'm watching out for that. Which way should you say he'd head, Mr. Cole?"

"Inland," said I, lying on the spur of the moment, I knew not why. "Try at the cottage where I've been staying."

"We have a man posted there already. That woman is one of the gang, and we've got her safe. But I'll take your advice, and have that side scoured whilst I hang about the place."

And he walked through the house, and out the back way, at the officer's heels; meanwhile the man with the wounded arm was swaying where he sat from loss of blood, and I had to help him into the open air before at last I was free to return to poor Eva in her place of loathsome safety.

I had been so long, however, that her patience was exhausted, and as I returned to the library by one door, she entered by the other.

"I could bear it no longer. Tell me—the worst!"

"Three of them are dead."

"Which three?"

She had crossed to the other door, and would not have me shut it. So I stood between her and the hearth, on which lay the captain's corpse, with the hearthrug turned up on either side to cover it.

"Harris for one," said I. "Outside lie José and——"

"Quick! Quick!"

"Senhor Santos."

Her face was as though the name meant nothing to her.

"And Mr. Rattray?" she cried. "And Mr. Rattray——"

"Has escaped for the present. He seems to have cut his way through the police and got over the wall by a ladder they left behind them. They are scouring the country—Miss Denison! Eva! My poor love!"

She had broken down utterly in a second fit of violent weeping; and a second time I took her in my arms, and stood trying in my clumsy way to comfort her, as though she were a little child. A lamp was burning in the library, and I recognized the arm-chair which Rattray had drawn

My Great Hour

thence for me on the night of our dinner—the very night before! I led Eva back into the room, and I closed both doors. I supported my poor girl to the chair, and once more I knelt before her and took her hands in mine. My great hour was come at last: surely a happy omen that it was also the hour before the dawn.

"Cry your fill, my darling," I whispered, with the tears in my own voice. "You shall never have anything more to cry for in this world! God has been very good to us. He brought you to me, and me to you. He has rescued us for each other. All our troubles are over; cry your fill; you will never have another chance so long as I live, if only you will let me live for you. Will you, Eva? Will you? Will you?"

She drew her hands from mine, and sat upright in the chair, looking at me with round eyes; but mine were dim; astonishment was all that I could read in her look, and on I went headlong, with growing impetus and passion.

"I know I am not much, my darling; but you know I was not always what my luck, good and bad, has left me now, and you will make a new man of me so soon! Besides, God must mean it, or He would not have thrown us together amid such horrors, and brought us through them together

235

Dead Men Tell No Tales

still. And you have no one else to take care of
you in the world! Won't you let me try, Eva?
Say that you will!"

"Then—you—love me?" she said slowly, in
a low, awe-struck voice that might have told me
my fate at once; but I was shaking all over in
the intensity of my passion, and for the moment
it was joy enough to be able at last to tell her all.

"Love you?" I echoed. "With every fibre of
my being! With every atom of my heart and
soul and body! I love you well enough to live
to a hundred for you, or to die for you to-night!"

"Well enough to—give me up?" she whispered.

I felt as though a cold hand had checked my
heart at its hottest, but I mastered myself sufficiently to face her question and to answer it as
honestly as I might.

"Yes!" I cried; "well enough even to do that,
if it was for your happiness; but I might be rather
difficult to convince about that."

"You are very strong and true," she murmured. "Yes, I can trust you as I have never
trusted anybody else! But—how long have you
been so foolish?" And she tried very hard to
smile.

"Since I first saw you; but I only knew it on
236

My Great Hour

the night of the fire. Till that night I resisted it like an idiot. Do you remember how we used to argue? I rebelled so against my love! I imagined that I had loved once already and once for all. But on the night of the fire I knew that my love for you was different from all that had gone before or would ever come again. I gave in to it at last, and oh! the joy of giving in! I had fought against the greatest blessing of my life, and I never knew it till I had given up fighting. What did I care about the fire? I was never happier—until now! You sang through my heart like the wind through the rigging; my one fear was that I might go to the bottom without telling you my love. When I asked to say a few last words to you on the poop, it was to tell you my love before we parted, that you might know I loved you whatever came. I didn't do so, because you seemed so frightened, poor darling! I hadn't it in my heart to add to your distress. So I left you without a word. But I fought the sea for days together simply to tell you what I couldn't die without telling you. When they picked me up, it was your name that brought back my senses after days of delirium. When I heard that you were dead, I longed to die myself. And when I found you lived after all, the horror of your surroundings was nothing to be compared with the mere fact that you lived; that you were unhappy and in danger was my only grief, but it was nothing to the thought of your death; and that I had to wait twenty-four hours without coming to you drove me nearer to madness than ever I was on the hen-coop. That's how I love you, Eva," I concluded; "that's how I love and will love you, for ever and ever, no matter what happens."

Those sweet gray eyes of hers had been fixed very steadily upon me all through this outburst; as I finished they filled with tears, and my poor love sat wringing her slender fingers, and upbraiding herself as though she were the most heartless coquette in the country.

"How wicked I am!" she moaned. "How ungrateful I must be! You offer me the unselfish love of a strong, brave man. I cannot take it. I have no love to give you in return."

"But some day you may," I urged, quite happily in my ignorance. "It will come. Oh, surely it will come, after all that we have gone through together!"

She looked at me very steadily and kindly through her tears.

"It has come, in a way," said she; "but it is

not your way, Mr. Cole. I do love you for your bravery and your—love—but that will not quite do for either of us."

"Why not?" I cried in an ecstasy. "My darling, it will do for me! It is more than I dared to hope for; thank God, thank God, that you should care for me at all!"

She shook her head.

"You do not understand," she whispered.

"I do. I do. You do not love me as you want to love."

"As I *could* love——"

"And as you will! It will come. It will come. I'll bother you no more about it now. God knows I can afford to leave well alone! I am only too happy—too thankful—as it is!"

And indeed I rose to my feet every whit as joyful as though she had accepted me on the spot. At least she had not rejected me; nay, she confessed to loving me in a way. What more could a lover want? Yet there was a dejection in her drooping attitude which disconcerted me in the hour of my reward. And her eyes followed me with a kind of stony remorse which struck a chill to my bleeding heart.

I went to the door; the hall was still empty, and I shut it again with a shudder at what I saw

before the hearth, at all that I had forgotten in
the little library. As I turned, another door
opened—the door made invisible by the multitude
of books around and upon it—and young Squire
Rattray stood between my love and me.

His clear, smooth skin was almost as pale as
Eva's own, but pale brown, the tint of rich ivory.
His eyes were preternaturally bright. And they
never glanced my way, but flew straight to Eva,
and rested on her very humbly and sadly, as her
two hands gripped the arms of the chair, and she
leant forward in horror and alarm.

"How could you come back?" she cried. "I
was told you had escaped!"

"Yes, I got away on one of their horses."

"I pictured you safe on board!"

"I very nearly was."

"Then why are you here?"

"To get your forgiveness before I go."

He took a step forward; her eyes and mine
were riveted upon him; and I still wonder which
of us admired him the more, as he stood there in
his pride and his humility, gallant and young,
and yet shamefaced and sad.

"You risk your life—for my forgiveness?"
whispered Eva at last.

"Risk it? I'll give myself up if you'll take

back some of the things you said to me—last night—and before."

There was a short pause.

"Well, you are not a coward, at all events!"

"Nor a murderer, Eva!"

"God forbid."

"Then forgive me for everything else that I have been—to you!"

And he was on his knees where I had knelt scarce a minute before; nor could I bear to watch them any longer. I believed that he loved her in his own way as sincerely as I did in mine. I believed that she detested him for the detestable crime in which he had been concerned. I believed that the opinion of him which she had expressed to his face, in my hearing, was her true opinion, and I longed to hear her mitigate it ever so little before he went. He won my sympathy as a gallant who valued a kind word from his mistress more than life itself. I hoped earnestly that that kind word would be spoken. But I had no desire to wait to hear it. I felt an intruder. I would leave them alone together for the last time.

So I walked to the door, but, seeing a key in it, I changed my mind, and locked it on the inside. In the hall I might become the unintentional in-

Dead Men Tell No Tales

strument of the squire's capture, though, so far as my ears served me, it was still empty as we had left it. I preferred to run no risks, and would have a look at the subterranean passage instead.

"I advise you to speak low," I said, "and not to be long. The place is alive with the police. If they hear you all will be up."

Whether *he* heard *me* I do not know. I left him on his knees still, and Eva with her face hidden in her hands.

The cellar was a strange scene to revisit within an hour of my deliverance from that very torture-chamber. It had been something more before I left it, but in it I could think only of the first occupant of the camp-stool. The lantern still burned upon the floor. There was the mattress, still depressed where I had lain face to face with insolent death. The bullet was in the plaster; it could not have missed by the breadth of many hairs. In the corner was the shallow grave, dug by Harris for my elements. And Harris was dead. And Santos was dead. But life and love were mine.

I would have gone through it all again!

And all at once I was on fire to be back in the library; so much so, that half a minute at the manhole, lantern in hand, was enough for me;

My Great Hour

and a mere funnel of moist brown earth—a terribly low arch propped with beams—as much as I myself ever saw of the subterranean conduit between Kirby House and the sea. But I understood that the curious may traverse it for themselves to this day on payment of a very modest fee.

As for me, I returned as I had come after (say) five minutes' absence; my head full once more of Eva, and of impatient anxiety for the wild young squire's final flight; and my heart still singing with the joy of which my beloved's kindness seemed a sufficient warranty. Poor egotist! Am I to tell you what I found when I came up those steep stairs to the chamber where I had left him on his knees to her? Or can you guess?

He was on his knees no more, but he held her in his arms, and as I entered he was kissing the tears from her wet, flushed cheek. Her eyelids drooped; she was pale as the dead without, so pale that her eyebrows looked abnormally and dreadfully dark. She did not cling to him. Neither did she resist his caresses, but lay passive in his arms as though her proper paradise was there. And neither heard me enter; it was as though they had forgotten all the world but one another.

Dead Men Tell No Tales

"So this is it," said I very calmly. I can hear my voice as I write.

They fell apart on the instant. Rattray glared at me, yet I saw that his eyes were dim. Eva clasped her hands before her, and looked me steadily in the face. But never a word.

"You love him?" I said sternly.

The silence of consent remained unbroken.

"Villain as he is?" I burst out.

And at last Eva spoke.

"I loved him before he was one," said she. "We were engaged."

She looked at him standing by, his head bowed, his arms folded; next moment she was very close to me, and fresh tears were in her eyes. But I stepped backward, for I had had enough.

"Can you not forgive me?"

"Oh, dear, yes."

"Can't you understand?"

"Perfectly," said I.

"You know you said——"

"I have said so many things!"

"But this was that you—you loved me well enough to—give me up."

And the silly ego in me—the endless and incorrigible I—imagined her pouting for a withdrawal of those brave words.

My Great Hour

"I not only said it," I declared, "but I meant every word of it."

None the less had I to turn from her to hide my anguish. I leaned my elbows on the narrow stone chimney-piece, which, with the grate below and a small mirror above, formed an almost solitary oasis in the four walls of books. In the mirror I saw my face; it was wizened, drawn, old before its time, and merely ugly in its sore distress, merely repulsive in its bloody bandages. And in the mirror also I saw Rattray, handsome, romantic, audacious, all that I was not, nor ever would be, and I "understood" more than ever, and loathed my rival in my heart

I wheeled round on Eva. I was not going to give her up—to him. I would tell her so before him—tell him so to his face. But she had turned away; she was listening to some one else. Her white forehead glistened. There were voices in the hall.

"Mr. Cole! Mr. Cole! Where are you, Mr. Cole?"

I moved over to the locked door. My hand found the key. I turned round with evil triumph in my heart, and God knows what upon my face. Rattray did not move. With lifted hands the girl was merely begging him to go, by the door that was open, down the stair. He shook his head grimly. With an oath I was upon them.

"Go, both of you!" I whispered hoarsely. "Now—while you can—and I can let you. Now! Now!

Still Rattray hung back.

I saw him glancing wistfully at my great revolver lying on the table under the lamp. I thrust it upon him, and pushed him towards the door.

"You go first. She shall follow. You will not grudge me one last word? Yes, I will take your hand. If you escape—be good to her!"

He was gone. Without, there was a voice still calling me; but now it sounded overhead.

"Good-by, Eva, I said. "You have not a moment to lose."

Yet those divine eyes lingered on my ugliness.

"You are in a very great hurry," said she, in the sharp little voice of her bitter moments.

"You love him; that is enough."

"And you, too!" she cried. "And you, too!"

And her pure, warm arms were round my neck; another instant, and she would have kissed me, she! I know it. I knew it then. But it was more than I would bear. As a brother! I had heard that tale before. Back I stepped again, all the man in me rebelling.

"That's impossible," said I rudely.

"It isn't. It's true. I do love you—for this!"

God knows how I looked!

"And I mayn't say good-by to you," she whispered. "And—and I love you—for that!"

"Then you had better choose between us," said I.

CHAPTER XX

THE STATEMENT OF FRANCIS RATTRAY

IN the year 1858 I received a bulky packet bearing the stamp of the Argentine Republic, a realm in which, to the best of my belief, I had not a solitary acquaintance. The superscription told me nothing. In my relations with Rattray his handwriting had never come under my observation. Judge then of my feelings when the first thing I read was his signature at the foot of the last page.

For five years I had been uncertain whether he was alive or dead. I had heard nothing of him from the night we parted in Kirby Hall. All I knew was that he had escaped from England and the English police; his letter gave no details of the incident. It was an astonishing letter; my breath was taken on the first close page; at the foot of it the tears were in my eyes. And all that part I must pass over without a word. I have never shown it to man or woman. It is sacred between man and man.

But the letter possessed other points of interest

The Statement of Francis Rattray

—of almost universal interest—to which no such scruples need apply; for it cleared up certain features of the foregoing narrative which had long been mysteries to all the world; and it gave me what I had tried in vain to fathom all these years, some explanation, or rather history, of the young Lancastrian's complicity with Joaquin Santos in the foul enterprise of the *Lady Jermyn*. And these passages I shall reproduce word for word; partly because of their intrinsic interest; partly for such new light as they may throw on this or that phase of the foregoing narrative; and, lastly, out of fairness to (I hope) the most gallant and most generous youth who ever slipped upon the lower slopes of Avernus.

Wrote Rattray:

"You wondered how I could have thrown in my lot with such a man. You may wonder still, for I never yet told living soul. I pretended I had joined him of my own free will. That was not quite the case. The facts were as follows:

"In my teens (as I think you know) I was at sea. I took my second mate's certificate at twenty, and from that to twenty-four my voyages were far between and on my own account. I had given way to our hereditary passion for smuggling. I

249

Dead Men Tell No Tales

kept a 'yacht' in Morecambe Bay, and more French brandy than I knew what to do with in my cellars. It was exciting for a time, but the excitement did not last. In 1851 the gold fever broke out in Australia. I shipped to Melbourne as third mate on a barque, and I deserted for the diggings in the usual course. But I was never a successful digger. I had little luck and less patience, and I have no doubt that many a good haul has been taken out of claims previously abandoned by me; for of one or two I had the mortification of hearing while still in the Colony. I suppose I had not the temperament for the work. Dust would not do for me—I must have nuggets. So from Bendigo I drifted to the Ovens, and from the Ovens to Ballarat. But I did no more good on one field than on another, and eventually, early in 1853, I cast up in Melbourne again with the intention of shipping home in the first vessel. But there were no crews for the homeward-bounders, and while waiting for a ship my little stock of gold dust gave out. I became destitute first—then desperate. Unluckily for me, the beginning of '53 was the hey-day of Captain Melville, the notorious bushranger. He was a young fellow of my own age. I determined to imitate his exploits. I could make nothing out there from

The Statement of Francis Rattray

an honest life; rather than starve I would lead a dishonest one. I had been born with lawless tendencies; from smuggling to bushranging was an easy transition, and about the latter there seemed to be a gallantry and romantic swagger which put it on the higher plane of the two. But I was not born to be a bushranger either. I failed at the very first attempt. I was outwitted by my first victim, a thin old gentleman riding a cob at night on the Geelong road.

" 'Why rob me?' said he. 'I have only ten pounds in my pocket, and the punishment will be the same as though it were ten thousand.'

" 'I want your cob,' said I (for I was on foot); 'I'm a starving Jack, and as I can't get a ship I'm going to take to the bush.'

"He shrugged his shoulders.

" 'To starve there?' said he. 'My friend, it is a poor sport, this bushranging. I have looked into the matter on my own account. You not only die like a dog, but you live like one too. It is not worth while. No crime is worth while under five figures, my friend. A starving Jack, eh? Instead of robbing me of ten pounds, why not join me and take ten thousand as your share of our first robbery? A sailor is the very man I want!'

Dead Men Tell No Tales

"I told him that what I wanted was his cob, and that it was no use his trying to hoodwink me by pretending he was one of my sort, because I knew very well that he was not; at which he shrugged again, and slowly dismounted, after offering me his money, of which I took half. He shook his head, telling me I was very foolish, and I was coolly mounting (for he had never offered me the least resistance), with my pistols in my belt, when suddenly I heard one cocked behind me.

"'Stop!' said he. 'It's my turn! Stop, or I shoot you dead!' The tables were turned, and he had me at his mercy as completely as he had been at mine. I made up my mind to being marched to the nearest police-station. But nothing of the kind. I had misjudged my man as utterly as you misjudged him a few months later aboard the *Lady Jermyn.* He took me to his house on the outskirts of Melbourne, a weatherboard bungalow, scantily furnished, but comfortable enough. And there he seriously repeated the proposal he had made me off-hand in the road. Only he put it a little differently. Would I go to the hulks for attempting to rob him of five pounds, or would I stay and help him commit a robbery, of which my share alone would be ten or fifteen thousand? You know which I chose.

The Statement of Francis Rattray

You know who this man was. I said I would join him. He made me swear it. And then he told me what his enterprise was: there is no need for me to tell you; nor indeed had it taken definite shape at this time. Suffice it that Santos had wind that big consignments of Austrailian gold were shortly to be shipped home to England; that he, like myself, had done nothing on the diggings, where he had looked to make his fortune, and out of which he meant to make it still.

"It was an extraordinary life that we led in the bungalow, I the guest, he the host, and Eva the unsuspecting hostess and innocent daughter of the house. Santos had failed on the fields, but he had succeeded in making valuable friends in Melbourne. Men of position and of influence spent their evenings on our veranda, among others the Melbourne agent for the *Lady Jermyn,* the likeliest vessel then lying in the harbor, and the one to which the first consignment of gold-dust would be entrusted if only a skipper could be found to replace the deserter who took you out. Santos made up his mind to find one. It took him weeks, but eventually he found Captain Harris on Bendigo, and Captain Harris was his man. More than that he was the man for the agent; and the *Lady Jermyn* was once more made ready for sea.

Dead Men Tell No Tales

Now began the complications. Quite openly, Santos had bought the schooner *Spindrift*, freighted her with wool, given me the command, and vowed that he would go home in her rather than wait any longer for the *Lady Jermyn*. At the last moment he appeared to change his mind, and I sailed alone as many days as possible in advance of the ship, as had been intended from the first; but it went sorely against the grain when the time came. I would have given anything to have backed out of the enterprise. Honest I might be no longer; I was honestly in love with Eva Denison. Yet to have backed out would have been one way of losing her for ever. Besides, it was not the first time I had run counter to the law, I who came of a lawless stock; but it would be the first time I had deserted a comrade or broken faith with one. I would do neither. In for a penny, in for a pound.

"But before my God I never meant it to turn out as it did, though I admit and have always admitted that my moral responsibility is but little if any the less on that account. Yet I was never a consenting party to wholesale murder, whatever else I was. The night before I sailed, Santos and the captain were aboard with me till the small hours. They promised me that every soul should

have every chance; that nothing but unforeseen
accident could prevent the boats from making
Ascension again in a matter of hours; that as long
as the gig was supposed to be lost with all hands,
nothing else mattered. So they promised, and
that Harris meant to keep his promise I fully
believe. That was not a wanton ruffian; but the
other would spill blood like water, as I told you
at the hall, and as no man now knows better than
yourself. He was notorious even in Portuguese
Africa on account of his atrocious treatment of
the blacks. It was a favorite boast of his that he
once poisoned a whole village; and that he himself tampered with the *Lady Jermyn's* boats you
can take my word, for I have heard him describe
how he left it to the last night, and struck the
blows during the applause at the concert on the
quarter-deck. He said it might have come out
about the gold in the gig, during the fire. It was
safer to run no risks.

"The same thing came into play aboard the
schooner. Never shall I forget the horror of that
voyage after Santos came aboard! I had a crew
of eight hands all told, and two he brought with
him in the gig. Of course they began talking
about the gold; they would have their share or
split when they got ashore; and there was mutiny

in the air, with the steward and the quarter-master of the *Lady Jermyn* for ring-leaders. Santos nipped it in the bud with a vengeance! He and Harris shot every man of them dead, and two who were shot through the heart they washed and dressed and set adrift to rot in the gig with false papers! God knows how we made Madeira; we painted the old name out and a new name in, on the way; and we shipped a Portuguese crew, not a man of whom could speak English. We shipped them aboard the Duque de Mondejo's yacht *Braganza;* the schooner *Spindrift* had disappeared from the face of the waters for ever. And with the men we took in plenty of sour claret and cigarettes; and we paid them well; and the Portuguese sailor is not inquisitive under such conditions.

"And now, honestly, I wished I had put a bullet through my head before joining in this murderous conspiracy; but retreat was impossible, even if I had been the man to draw back after going so far; and I had a still stronger reason for standing by the others to the bitter end. I could not leave our lady to these ruffians. On the other hand, neither could I take her from them, for (as you know) she justly regarded me as the most flagrant ruffian of them all. It was in me and

He and Harris shot every man of them dead.

through me that she was deceived, insulted, humbled, and contaminated; that she should ever have forgiven me for a moment is more than I can credit or fathom to this hour. . . . So there we were. She would not look at me. And I would not leave her until death removed me. Santos had been kind enough to her hitherto; he had been kind enough (I understand) to her mother before her. It was only in the execution of his plans that he showed his Napoleonic disregard for human life; and it was precisely herein that I began to fear for the girl I still dared to love. She took up an attitude as dangerous to her safety as to our own. She demanded to be set free when we came to land. Her demand was refused. God forgive me, it had no bitterer opponent than myself! And all we did was to harden her resolution; that mere child threatened us to our faces, never shall I forget the scene! You know her spirit: if we would not set her free, she would tell all when we landed. And you remember how Santos used to shrug? That was all he did then. It was enough for me who knew him. For days I never left them alone together. Night after night I watched her cabin door. And she hated me the more for never leaving her alone! I had to resign myself to that.

Dead Men Tell No Tales

"The night we anchored in Falmouth Bay, thinking then of taking our gold straight to the Bank of England, as eccentric lucky diggers— that night I thought would be the last for one or other of us. He locked her in her cabin. He posted himself outside on the settee. I sat watching him across the table. Each had a hand in his pocket, each had a pistol in that hand, and there we sat, with our four eyes locked, while Harris went ashore for papers. He came back in great excitement. What with stopping at Madeira, and calms, and the very few knots we could knock out of the schooner at the best of times, we had made a seven or eight weeks' voyage of it from Ascension—where, by the way, I had arrived only a couple of days before the *Lady Jermyn*, though I had nearly a month's start of her. Well, Harris came back in the highest state of excitement: and well he might: the papers were full of *you*, and of the burning of the *Lady Jermyn!*

"Now mark what happened. You know, of course, as well as I do; but I wonder if you can even yet realize what it was to us! Our prisoner hears that you are alive, and she turns upon Santos and tells him he is welcome to silence her, but it will do us no good now, as *you* know that the

258

ship was wilfully burned, and with what object. It is the single blow she can strike in self-defence; but a shrewder one could scarcely be imagined. She *had* talked to you, at the very last; and by that time she did know the truth. What more natural than that she should confide it to you? She had had time to tell you enough to hang the lot of us; and you may imagine our consternation on hearing that she had told you all she knew! From the first we were never quite sure whether to believe it or not. That the papers breathed no suspicion of foul play was neither here nor there. Scotland Yard might have seen to that. Then we read of the morbid reserve which was said to characterize all your utterances concerning the *Lady Jermyn*. What were we to do? What we no longer dared to do was to take our gold-dust straight to the Bank. What we did, you know.

"We ran round to Morecambe Bay, and landed the gold as we Rattrays had landed lace and brandy from time immemorial. We left Eva in charge of Jane Braithwaite, God only knows how much against my will, but we were in a corner, it was life or death with us, and to find out how much you knew was a first plain necessity. And the means we took were the only means in our

power; nor shall I say more to you on that subject
than I said five years ago in my poor old house.
That is still the one part of the whole conspiracy
of which I myself am most ashamed.

"And now it only remains for me to tell you
why I have written all this to you, at such great
length, so long after the event. My wife wished
it. The fact is that she wants you to think better
of me than I deserve; and I—yes—I confess that
I should like you not to think quite as ill of me
as you must have done all these years. I was
villain enough, but do not think I am unpun-
ished.

"I am an outlaw from my country. I am morally
a transported felon. Only in this no-man's land
am I a free man; let me but step across the border
and I am worth a little fortune to the man who
takes me. And we have had a hard time here,
though not so hard as I deserved; and the hardest
part of all. . . ."

But you must guess the hardest part: for the
letter ended as it began, with sudden talk of his
inner life, and tentative inquiry after mine. In
its entirety, as I say, I have never shown it to a
soul; there was just a little more that I read to
my wife (who could not hear enough about his);

then I folded up the letter, and even she has never seen the passages to which I allude.

And yet I am not one of those who hold that the previous romances of married people should be taboo between them in after life. On the contrary, much mutual amusement, of an innocent character, may be derived from a fair and free interchange upon the subject; and this is why we, in our old age (or rather in mine), find a still unfailing topic in the story of which Eva Denison was wayward heroine and Frank Rattray the nearest approach to a hero. Sometimes these reminiscences lead to an argument; for it has been the fate of my life to become attached to argumentative persons. I suppose because I myself hate arguing. On the day that I received Rattray's letter we had one of our warmest discussions. I could repeat every word of it after forty years.

"A good man does not necessarily make a good husband," I innocently remarked.

"Why do you say that?" asked my wife, who never would let a generalization pass unchallenged.

"I was thinking of Rattray," said I. "The most tolerant of judges could scarcely have described him as a good man five years ago. Yet

Dead Men Tell No Tales

I can see that he has made an admirable husband. On the whole, and if you can't be both, it is better to be the good husband!"

It was this point that we debated with so much ardor. My wife would take the opposite side; that is her one grave fault. And I must introduce personalities; that, of course, is among the least of mine. I compared myself with Rattray, as a husband, and (with some sincerity) to my own disparagement. I pointed out that he was an infinitely more fascinating creature, which was no hard saying, for that epithet at least I have never earned. And yet it was the word to sting my wife.

"Fascinating, perhaps!" said she. "Yes, that is the very word; but—fascination is not love!"

And then I went to her, and stroked her hair (for she had hung her head in deep distress), and kissed the tears from her eyes. And I swore that her eyes were as lovely as Eva Denison's, that there seemed even more gold in her glossy brown hair, that she was even younger to look at. And at the last and craftiest compliment my own love looked at me through her tears, as though some day or other she might forgive me.

"Then why did you want to give me up to him?" said she.